AND baby MAKES TWO

Dyan Sheldon

WALKER BOOKS

This is a work of fiction. Names, characters, places and incidents
are either the product of the author's imagination or, if real, are used
fictitiously. All statements, activities, stunts, descriptions, information
and material of any other kind contained herein are included for
entertainment purposes only and should not be relied on for
accuracy or replicated as they may result in injury.

First published 2000 by Walker Books Ltd
87 Vauxhall Walk, London SE11 5HJ

This edition published 2010

2 4 6 8 10 9 7 5 3

This book has been typeset in Sabon

Printed and bound in Great Britain by Clays Ltd, St Ives plc

British Library Cataloguing in Publication Data:
a catalogue record for this book is available from the British Library

ISBN 978-1-4063-1548-6

www.walker.co.uk

When I Grow Up

In many ways, the twenty-fifth of October was an ordinary day, which means it started with a fight with my mother and carried on from there.

The fight with my mother was because there wasn't any milk for the tea. As per usual, this was my fault. Nothing was ever Hilary's fault. God knows what she did before she had me to blame for everything. Because of the fight, I was late for school again. Mr Cox, my tutor, gave me a detention. I tried to reason with him.

"But it's my birthday," I said. "You can't give me a detention on my birthday. That's Fascism."

"No it isn't," said Mr Cox. "It's frustration. But you can do the detention on Monday." He gave me his cheesy, I'm-your-friend smile. "Happy Birthday."

After that I got told off for talking in geography. Then I got told off for talking in maths. Then I got told off for not having my homework in history. Then I got told off for not having my homework in English. And, finally, I got told off by the headteacher for talking back to my geography teacher. All systems normal.

I never let that stuff bother me too much, though. I mean, it was life, wasn't it? I knew what preachers (teachers and parents) were like. I couldn't remember a time when I didn't hate my mother, except maybe when I was really little and didn't know any better. And school was never my thing, either. My best lesson at school was lunch. I was really good at lunch. I was enthusiastic, paid attention, tried hard and never gave the dinner ladies any lip. If they'd given out marks for lunch, I would've been top of the class. But my standards weren't as high in my other subjects. In my other subjects I was bottom of the class, unless I'd been sent to the headteacher and wasn't actually *in* the class. No one ever asked me what I'd got in a test unless they'd done really badly and wanted to find someone who had done worse.

Even if I had let that stuff bother me, though, it wouldn't have bothered me that day. It wasn't just my birthday. It was my fifteenth birthday! One more year down!

All I'd ever wanted to be was grown up. Then nobody could boss me around and I could do what I pleased. The age I really wanted to be was sixteen, of course, when you can legally do things without getting someone's permission, but fifteen was pretty close. Adulthood was shining like a beacon in front of me only twelve months away.

I usually walked home from school with my best friend, Shanee, but since Shanee was away and it was my birthday *and* raining I took the bus. I sat right at the back in the corner, where no old lady would hit me with her shopping or glare at me to give up my seat. I put my headphones on and stared out the window. I didn't care what the other passengers thought, I sang along with my Discman all the way home. I was that happy.

Listening to my Discman and watching the street from the bus was one of my favourite pastimes. It was like a film. You know, like the bits between the talking when there's just music and people doing stuff. Sometimes *I* was in the film, and sometimes I was just watching it, making up stories about the people I saw.

Today, since it was my birthday, I was in the film.

The camera watched me watching the shoppers hurrying through the rain. I had Garbage on my Discman.

"When I Grow Up" was my favourite song.

There were tons of women with plastic-covered pushchairs in the street. They looked like they were pushing bubbles filled with babies. The bus stopped in front of McDonald's. There were more women with pushchairs sitting together in the window, talking and laughing while their children mashed up chips and played with the toy of the week.

The camera came in close on my face as I watched

them and stayed on me as I imagined myself sitting with the women in McDonald's, a shopping list in my pocket, joking about my husband, knowing exactly what I had to do for the rest of my life.

I got so involved in thinking about what kind of pushchair I would buy for my kid that I missed my stop. I got out at the next one and walked back.

If I really was in a film, when I got home the flat would've been filled with balloons and everybody would've been there, wearing party hats and hiding behind the sofa to surprise me. But I wasn't in a film. At least not that one. The flat was empty: no party and no balloons. I'd already opened all my presents and cards and my mother wouldn't be back from work for a couple of hours. This was fine with me. All she ever did was yell and nag. You'd think she was permanently suffering from PMT the way she carried on.

Anyway, I didn't care that there was no one there because I needed extra time to get ready. My mum and her boyfriend, Charley, were taking me to Planet Hollywood for dinner. This was a big deal, since Hilary and Charley's normal idea of splashing out was to eat at Pizza Hut, damn the expense.

I'd wanted to go to Planet Hollywood since it opened. I reckoned you never knew who you'd bump into in a place like that. The brainboxes at school all wanted to go to university and become professors or solicitors and stuff like that, but I wanted to get married and have my own flat and lots of children. That was my true ambition. As far as I was concerned, having a family was the outfit you wore in life and everything else – jobs and stuff – were just the accessories. I even went through a phase when I was younger of designing my dream home and family with pictures from magazines. I bought dozens of cheap photo albums and filled them up with pictures of houses and husbands and children. They were all still under my bed.

But I wasn't stupid. I knew that before I could get married, I had to have a boyfriend. A *real* boy-friend. I modelled myself on the Alicia Silverstone character in *Clueless*: I didn't go out with school-boys. Schoolboys were pimply and immature. They played air guitars and had food fights that made them gasp with laughter and disgusted everyone else. But having a rule about not going out with schoolboys meant I lost out. So far I hadn't really gone out with anyone.

That's why I was pretty excited about Planet Hollywood. It was the kind of place where I might meet someone I *could* go out with. I knew from films that it was when you went somewhere you didn't usually go that your life could change. And I definitely wanted my life to change.

I threw my wet clothes over the radiator and put on the stereo. My mother was still recovering from the break-up of Genesis. She thought the music I liked should be played just below a whisper and several miles away. So since she wasn't there to complain, I put it on really loud. Mrs Mugurdy upstairs immediately started pounding on the ceiling, but, as per usual, I pretended I didn't hear her.

I was really looking forward to my bath. I wanted to have a long soak and shave my legs and stuff like that in peace and quiet. Which was something I couldn't do when the old bag was home. She'd be banging on the bathroom door all the time, shrieking at me to hurry up, didn't I know that other people needed to use the loo, too?

I put the kettle on and went to run the water. It took me a while to go through all my oil balls and bubbles, choosing just the right one for the occasion. Normally I used Raspberry Ripple from the Body Shop, but tonight was special. Like the kid in the Garbage song, I was going to turn every table I could get my hands on.

I wanted something grown-up and sexy, so if someone interesting *was* at Planet Hollywood, he'd be sure to notice me. I finally decided on White Musk. I read that White Musk was Sharon Stone's favourite. I reckoned if it was good enough for Sharon Stone, it was good enough for me.

The automatic switch on the kettle didn't work, of course, so it was nearly dry by the time I remembered that I'd left it on.

"Thank you, God," I said to the ceiling as I refilled it. If I burned out one more kettle my mother would kill me.

While the second kettle was boiling, I lit some candles and incense (to help me relax), and picked

10

out a CD to play while I was in the bath. My nan sent me a voucher for Tower Records for my birthday. My nan loves music. She stopped listening to anything new in about 1948, but she was in favour of it as a general principle. I got two new CDs with her token: the soundtrack to *Titanic* and the soundtrack to *The Bodyguard*. I put on *Titanic*. *Titanic* was my favourite film that year.

I lay in the bath with the light out and the candles flickering, and forgot about school and my mother and my dreary, boring life. I rewrote *Titanic* in my head. Instead of Jack dying in the sea and Rose ending up as an old lady who could hardly walk, they both drifted off on a door and ended up on a deserted island. The water was blue-green and palm trees swayed in a gentle breeze. We ate coconuts and bananas and Jack caught fish with his bare hands. It was paradise. Just the two of us, with no one else to push us around. I closed my eyes and I was making love to Jack on the white sand in the moonlight. Since I'd never been out with anyone, I'd never actually made love, of course, but I'd seen enough films to get the general idea. His kisses were electric. He looked down at me in the cool white shine of the moon. My body glistened with sand.

"You don't need jewels, Rose," Jack whispered. "You're beautiful as you are..."

The moist, full lips, soft as cotton balls moved towards mine.

A sudden furious banging on the bathroom door

11

interrupted our kiss.

I froze with my face in the duck sponge. I hadn't even heard her come in.

"Lana?" my mother bawled. "Lana, are you going to be out of there soon? I need to go to the toilet."

I'd blown all my birthday money on a new outfit that was special enough for Planet Hollywood. It was absolutely fabulous. The dress was silky and black, with thin straps dotted with rhinestones and a rhinestone heart on the left breast. I saw Julia Roberts wearing something very similar on a chat show. The dress was so clingy that you couldn't wear *anything* underneath except really thin tights. I got silver tights in Sock Shop that were really thin but glittery, though not *too* glittery. Glittery like Cher would wear, not glittery like Baby Spice. And I bought this black lace jacket to go over the dress.

But the most expensive things I bought were the shoes. They were incredible. They were black and silver, with chunky six-inch heels, thick soles and ankle straps. They were the kind of shoes you'd wear if you were going to the Oscars. The old cow would have a fit if she knew how much I spent on those shoes.

I had some articles I'd cut out of magazines that showed you how to make yourself up like a model. I spread them out on my dressing-table with all my new make-up. Foundation, lipgloss, eye shadow, mascara, eyeliner – I had the lot in the trendiest autumn shades. I teetered in front of the mirror, trying to get my face just right. It's important to look natural, but more perfect than natural. One of the articles said you should dust a little talc on your lashes to hold the mascara better, but that didn't work too well. I got powder in my eyes and everything started running. I had to go back to the bathroom to wash it all off and start again.

Charley arrived straight from the garage while I was rubbing fresh Nivea into my skin. The old cow started banging on the door again.

"Lana!" she bellowed. "Lana, Charley needs a shower."

Knowing Charley, I reckoned what he really needed was dry-cleaning. I personally couldn't go out with a man who was covered in grease all the time. I was only going to date professionals.

"For God's sake!" I screamed back. "How am I supposed to get ready when you keep interrupting me?"

I threw the towel at the rack and staggered back to my room. I didn't have much experience with six-inch heels.

I was just choosing my perfume when she started screaming again.

"For the love of God, Lana! Do you think there's any chance we'll get out of the house tonight?"

"I'm coming… I'm coming…" I screamed back. "Just give me a minute, will you?"

I sprayed some Tommy Girl on my pulse points, put on my lace jacket, and studied myself in the mirror. I was knockout. Really knockout. I looked at least twenty. A twenty-year-old model, that's what I looked like.

I gave my reflection a sexy smile.

"Kate Winslet, eat your heart out," I whispered. "Eat your heart out, and choke."

My mother and Charley were in the kitchen, having a glass of wine while they waited for me. As per usual, they didn't offer me any. Not even on my birthday. My best friend Shanee's mother let her have a drink on special occasions, but the strongest thing Hilary Spiggs would let me have was Diet Coke.

I walked slowly down the hall, trying not to sway too much.

"Here I am," I called as I reached the door. I tossed my hair and smiled shyly. Like Cher in *Moonstruck* when she's had her make-over and she sees Nicolas Cage waiting for her, wondering if he'll notice the difference. "All ready to go!"

In *Moonstruck*, Nicolas Cage is gobsmacked by the sight of Cher all dressed up with her hair in curls.

In my kitchen, my mum and Charley were pretty gobsmacked by the sight of me.

Charley was nearest the door.

"Wow," said Charley. "Look at you!" Then he started to say "Happy Birthday, Lana," but he only got as far as "Hap—"

She'd been staring at me in silence, more like a rabbit caught in the headlights than Nicolas Cage caught by love, and then she went off like a siren.

"What the hell are you supposed to be dressed up for?" she shrieked. "You're not going out with us, looking like *that*."

Charley glanced over at her. "Hilary," said Charley. "Hilary, don't start."

"Go right back to your room and take that junk off your face this minute!" she roared. "And put on something decent while you're at it."

"I am decent." My voice was as stiff as my eyelashes.

"Only if you're a child prostitute," she informed me. "We're not going anywhere with you dressed like a tart."

Charley knocked back his wine. "You look like you might be cold," he mumbled. "Have you got a coat?"

"Never mind the coat," she roared. "She isn't leaving this house like that, and that's final."

Charley looked at his glass in case it had been magically topped up since he emptied it.

Sometimes I didn't know why she put up with Charley. He was unattractive, overweight, filthy ninety-five per cent of the time, and he never wanted to do anything but go to the pub with his mates or watch telly. But sometimes I didn't know why he put up with *her*, with her nasty moods and everything. This was one of the times I felt sorry for him.

"For Christ's sake, Hil," said Charley. "It's Lana's birthday. Let her be."

My mother turned her glare from me to him. "It's her fifteenth birthday, not her thirtieth." She was pronouncing her words really clearly. She went back to glaring at me. "I'm your mother," she informed me.

Big news.

"So what?" I screamed back. "I'm not a little kid any more. You can't keep treating me like I'm a baby."

She gave me her Mother Face. The Mother Face wasn't pleasant and affectionate and understanding like the face of the mother in the Oxo ad. The Mother Face made it clear that *she* knew everything, and that she could say or do anything and it was all right because she once carried me around inside her for a couple of months. Big deal.

"I'm your mother," she said again. In case I'd forgotten in the two seconds since the last time she said it.

"Not 'cos you wanted to be!" I screamed. "You never wanted me." I knew this because I'd heard her talking to my nan about it when we went to Hastings in the summer. I was an accident. My sisters were already grown up; she'd really been planning to go back to college.

"What are you talking about? Of course I wanted you."

"No you didn't. You wanted to drink gin and throw yourself down the stairs."

She rolled her eyes and sighed.

"If you don't get that stuff off your face and put

16

on something decent, I'm going to drink gin and throw *you* down the stairs," said my mother.

"I'm fifteen," I said in my coldest, most grown-up voice. "Everybody my age dresses like this."

"Everybody your age does not live with *me*."

"I don't hear anybody crying."

She slammed her glass down on the counter. "As long as you live in this house, you do what I say. Now go back to your room and put on some clothes."

"No." My lower lip trembled. "I'm not changing, and you can't make me."

The old witch cackled. "Oh can't I?"

Charley said, "Hil, let it go, all right? She'll be sitting down anyway, what's the difference?" He gave me a weak smile. "You look really pretty."

She looked like she wanted to hit him.

"Stay out of this, Charley. This is my house and my daughter!" The glasses on the draining-board started to rattle as the decibel level rose. "I don't need any advice on bringing up children from *you*."

Charley gazed at the wine bottle with real longing, but it was behind her shoulder and he knew better than to try to make a grab for it.

"Hil, for Christ's sake. You're getting all wound up about nothing. Let's just get our coats and go, all right? Have a nice me—"

"I'm not going anywhere with her looking like that!" She was talking to him, but she was looking at me. "Am I making myself clear, Little Miss

Babe Power? You can have cheese on toast for your birthday dinner for all I care."

My teeth were clenched so tight I thought they might chip.

"That's fine with me!" I shrieked back. "The only place I'd go with you is your funeral, you miserable old cow."

That was when she hit me. Slap with her palm, right on the cheek.

"Don't you talk to me like that." She was shaking with rage. "I'm your mother."

I put my face right into hers. "Well, I bloody well wish you weren't. Do you hear me? I'd rather have Cruella De Vil as my mother!"

"The way you're going, you may get your wish!" shrieked the Wicked Witch.

And I ran out of the room and out of the flat as fast as a person on six-inch heels could.

Happy Birthday to Me

If I'd had somewhere to go, I'd've gone there.

But I didn't. We never saw my dad again after he left, so he was out. My half-sisters, Charlene and Dara, both lived south of the river, and my nan lived in Hastings, so they were out, too. So was Shanee, because even though she lived just down the road she'd gone away for the weekend.

I marched through the boring streets of north-west London on automatic.

I was back on the *Titanic*, pushing through the hysterical mobs, looking for Jack. I was wearing the bomber jacket he'd put around me. I was still soaked from the icy waves that broke across the ship as she sunk deeper and deeper into the endless water, but my soul was on fire. I would not die without seeing him one more time. "Jack!" screamed my heart. "Jack! Jack! Jack!"

A door blocked my way. I pushed it open with my last desperate burst of strength.

McDonald's was warm and bright. A pub would've been more suitable for my mood, but I was too young to go to a pub, of course. Yet another disadvantage of youth.

My dress was stuck to me like a wet tissue. It was like wearing nothing and a really tight, uncomfortable bodysuit at the same time. Blisters were already throbbing on my feet. But I didn't care. I didn't even glance at myself in the glass door as I marched through, that's how much I didn't care.

There were maybe a dozen people in the restaurant, including the bored-looking kids behind the counter. I strode through the empty tables as if I was going up to get my Oscar, but instead of an Oscar I got a Big Mac, large fries and a chocolate milkshake. None of those things are exactly great for your skin, but I didn't care about that just then either. What was the use of having good skin and knowing how to dress and wear make-up if you never had a chance to show yourself off a bit? There wasn't any use, that was what. If my mother had her way, I'd still be wearing a Babygro and sucking on a dummy.

I sat at a table by the window, so I'd have something to do besides cry while I ate.

Some bloody birthday.

McDonald's is all right, but it isn't Planet Hollywood. Without the mothers and children it was pretty dead. Like a film set between takes. And it was too bright, brighter than usual. It reminded me of a hospital. You know, all cheery with yellow walls and fluorescent lights so no one will notice that they're dying.

I turned my back on the hanging plants and the posters advertising the latest Disney blockbuster, and stared into the rain.

Happy Birthday to me, I thought as I took out my burger. Happy Birthday, dear Lana, Happy Birthday to me.

I bit into my Big Mac. It tasted like cardboard with ketchup and a slice of pickle on it.

A couple stopped on the other side of the window, trying to keep dry while they waited for a bus. They had their arms linked and he was holding the umbrella over her head. They looked really happy.

I felt like I was going to choke. I dropped my burger and bit my lip.

Don't cry, I told myself. Wait till you get back outside.

I'd never thought about it before, but I reckoned that was why people in songs were always walking in the rain, so nobody could tell that they were sobbing their hearts out.

I opened my tiny tub of ketchup and dipped a chip in it, thinking about all the other girls in the world whose birthday was on the twenty-fifth of October. They were having parties with all their friends laughing around them. They had heaps of presents and everybody was hugging them and telling them how terrific they looked. Their mothers loved them. Then I thought about a girl

I'd read about who died at her own birthday party. When I first read it I thought it was really sad and depressing, but just then, dripping in one corner of McDonald's, I would have changed places with her like a shot. I mean, so she was dead, so what? At least she'd had a good time. It was a lot better than dying of pneumonia with the smell of stale grease on your breath.

I stuck my straw in my milkshake and took a sip. The couple on the other side of the window were snogging. The umbrella banged against the glass.

I gave up and let the tears come. Sip … sip … gulp … gulp … sip … sip … gulp … gulp…

I felt like a trapped animal, as if no matter what I did I was never going to escape. I was always going to be Hilary Spiggs' little kid, being yelled at and told what to do.

I was crying so much that I didn't even know he was there, sitting at the table beside me.

And then I heard his voice.

I looked over, trying to suck back a few thousand tears.

He couldn't've been there long, because he hadn't even unwrapped his straw yet. He was leaning towards me, holding out a pocket packet of tissues. He looked embarrassed.

"Are you all right?" He jabbed the tissues in my direction. "Your—I—"

I couldn't speak.

Partly this was because I was trying to stop crying, but partly it was because of *him*. He wasn't

Leonardo DiCaprio, but he wasn't bad. He was tall, dark and slim. He didn't have spots, or wear glasses, or dress like his mother still bought his clothes. In fact, he was a pretty sharp dresser. I'd seen John Travolta on a chat show wearing a shirt almost the same shade of blue as his. And he was wearing a top-of-the-range Baby G. Plus, he was well over twenty. It was like *Sleepless in Seattle* the first time Tom Hanks' and Meg Ryan's eyes meet. It was a dream come true.

He leaned a bit closer, still waving the packet.

"Your make-up," he said. "I thought you might need these."

I was so touched by his incredible kindness and sensitivity that I nearly started crying again. I took a breath and smiled. It was the smile I always practised in the mirror: sunny but sexy. It was the best smile I had.

"Thanks." I kept the smile, but looked down at the table so he'd know I was shy and embarrassed, too, and not in the habit of having nervous breakdowns in public. "I'm sorry—"

Our fingers touched as I took the tissues from his hand. Maybe if they hadn't, I'd've mopped my eyes with his tissues and that would've been the end of it. But they did touch. Electricity shot through me. I didn't want him to go.

"It's my birthday," I snuffled. "I had a fight with my mum."

"Your birthday? Really?" He smiled. "Well, Happy Birthday—"

"Lana." I laughed and snuffled at the same time. "Lana Spiggs."

He held out his hand. "Les," he said. "Les Craft."

We just sort of stared at each other for a couple of seconds.

"So, which birthday is it?" he finally asked.

I didn't hesitate for even a nanosecond. I didn't want to put him off because he thought I was too young.

"My eighteenth."

He smiled. "Well, Happy Birthday, Lana Spiggs."

Happy Birthday to me.

Les Craft was twenty years old, kind, sensitive and intelligent (he had two A levels). He wasn't exactly a babe, but he was good-looking in a quiet way, and he had two gold hoops in his left ear, and he did dress very smart. Plus, there was no grease on his hands. Les was assistant manager of the Block-buster on the high street.

"I thought you looked familiar," I fibbed. I wanted him to know he was special, not some dork a girl would never notice. "I go in there all the time."

He smiled. In my opinion, Calvin Klein could've made millions if he bottled that smile.

"I know."

He'd noticed me! I couldn't believe it. I hadn't noticed him – I didn't really look at the boys who worked at Blockbuster because they tended to have bad skin and only recommend action films – but this attractive man had noticed *me*.

I told him all about my most recent fight with the Curse of Kilburn while we ate our burgers. He dipped his chips in the ketchup just like I did.

Les was very understanding. He had a mother, too.

"They have a lot of trouble letting go," said Les. "My mum's the worst. I won't let my mum in my flat, because she'd start tidying up the minute she got through the door." He smiled his break-your-heart smile. "And she's always after me to cut my hair."

"Oh, don't do that." It was long enough to hang sexily over his collar, but not so long that you'd mistake him for a girl from the back. "It's lovely."

Sunshine flooded McDonald's.

"OK. I'll tell my mum Lana likes it like this."

I felt like someone was pouring hot fudge sauce through my veins. *Lana likes it like this...* It was as though we'd known each other for ages. That had to mean that I'd see him again.

Les stuffed the chip packet and his napkin and the straw wrapper into his burger box. There wasn't one crumb or blob of ketchup at his place.

"I've got to get back to the shop," he said. He made it sound like he'd rather go anywhere else. "Do you want to come with me and hang out?"

I didn't have to think even once, never mind twice. "Yeah, sure."

Let the old bat worry that I'd been raped or run over by a car or something. It served her right.

Les took me home when he finished work. I couldn't believe my luck. He not only had a job and a flat (well, a room in a flat), he had a car. It wasn't a Porsche or a Jeep or anything cool like that, but it wasn't an old banger like Charley's van that you had to park on a hill so you could get it started the next day, either.

It had gone midnight by the time we got to my road. I made him let me off at the corner. In case she was hovering behind the curtains.

"Are you sure you'll be all right?" asked Les. "I could come in with you if you want."

He sounded really concerned.

"No, I'll be fine." I undid my seat belt and took hold of the door handle. "She isn't violent. She's just a pain."

The last thing I wanted was for him to meet Hilary. Women often end up looking just like their mothers. Oprah did a whole programme on it. What if Les took one look at *her*, decided that was what I was going to end up like, and I never saw him again? Plus, she'd be sure to tell him I was only fifteen. Probably before I'd even introduced him. "You know she's only fifteen," she'd say. "Do you want to go to prison?"

I pulled on the handle. "She'll be in bed now anyway," I lied. "It'll be all right."

Les grabbed my right hand.

When you're little, you think a lot about

26

whether or not you should kiss a boy on the first date. Will he think you're easy? Will he think you kiss every boy you meet like that? Will you catch something?

But since we hadn't technically been on our first date yet, I didn't worry about it. As soon as I felt his skin on mine I turned to face him. I'd practised kissing my pillow and stuff like that (so I'd know what to do), but kissing Les was not like kissing my pillow. His lips were warm, and soft as the centre of a chocolate cream. I was melting from within. I didn't even jump or gag or anything when he stuck his tongue in my mouth. It was hardly slimy at all.

"How about Sunday?" he whispered when we came up for air. "I've got to work Saturday and Sunday night, but we could do something in the afternoon. After lunch." He stroked my hair. "If you're not busy."

He had to be joking. I would never be busy again in my life.

She was waiting up for me, of course. She'd ruined the first part of my birthday for me, and now she was determined to ruin the last part as well. She must've sensed I was having a good time somewhere. I always said she was a witch.

She launched herself from the window as soon as she saw me come down the street and popped out of the living-room like a cuckoo in a clock as soon as I stepped into the hall.

"I'd like to talk to you," she said in this dead flat voice.

She was a bit drunk. Alcohol's meant to make you jolly, but she always gets really earnest and serious when she has a bit to drink.

I didn't meet her eyes. I wasn't going to let her spoil what had turned out to be the best night of my life. I was going to go to bed and pretend that Les was beside me, holding me tight, telling me how wonderful I was.

I locked the front door and marched past her.

"Lana. Did you hear me? We need to talk."

I opened the door to my room. "Talk to yourself," I said. "I'm going to bed."

"I'm your mother," she said. No one could ever accuse Hilary Spiggs of being original. "I think I have a right to know where you've been all night."

"Selling my body," I said. "Where else?"

I would've slammed the door in her face, but she'd wedged herself against the frame.

"Lana, look, I know I overreacted—"

She touched my shoulder. I jumped as if she'd stabbed me.

"Get your hands off me," I ordered.

She got her hands off me. She must've been more drunk than I thought, though, because she almost looked like she was going to cry.

"I'm sorry, Lana. I don't want things to be like this."

Maybe if I hadn't had the best birthday of my

life, and maybe if I hadn't realized I had enough power to make her cry, I would have broken down then and said I was sorry too, and everything would've been different. That's what I think now, at any rate. But it's not what I thought then. I didn't care that she was sorry. I was chuffed I could make her cry. And I didn't give a stuff what she wanted. I was like Dorothy in *The Wizard of Oz*, standing on the yellow brick road with the Emerald City shimmering in front of me. Only it wasn't the Emerald City I saw, it was my future. It was nearly six feet tall, had a tongue like a lizard's, and drove a Ford.

"Well, that's the way they are," I told her. And I gave her a shove that knocked her against the wall and slammed my door behind me.

My mother always told me that love wasn't like it is in films and songs and stuff like that. Meaning that it wasn't like that for her. Charlene and Dara's father died when they were little. Hard though it was to believe, the Spiggs had been madly in love with him. She married my father because he was the best she could get with two children and cellulite and her lousy personality. Charlene and Dara's father was God's gift to the earth; mine was a reminder that God likes to punish people.

"You don't just meet someone and BOOM, you're in love," my mother had told me. "Real life isn't like in films."

I didn't believe her when I was twelve, and now

that I was fifteen I knew she was lying. She wanted me to have the same miserable life she had, that's why.

Love was exactly like it was in films: BOOM.

One minute you're just an ordinary person, waiting for something great to happen, and the next minute – BOOM – something great has happened. You feel happier than you've ever felt before – than you ever thought you could feel.

I'm not sure if I fell in love with Les when he kissed me, or if it happened before that, when we were talking in McDonald's. Not that it mattered. I knew that first night that he was the man I'd been waiting for since I was born.

After she stopped shouting at me through the door and finally staggered off to her own room, I put a Celine Dion CD in my Discman and lay on my bed, staring at the glow-in-the-dark stars I'd stuck on the ceiling. I went over everything Les had said. I imagined every detail of his face, and the way he laughed, and the way he ate, and the way he drove, and the way he looked at me and how he tasted in my mouth.

So this is love, I thought. L-O-V-E: LOVE.

The CD ended and a really old song floated into my head. After my dad escaped when I was four, me and Hilary went to live with my nan for a few years. The Spiggs threw herself into rebuilding her life, so it was Nan I spent time with. Most afternoons we'd get out her box of old records and we'd play them on her ancient record player. This song was one of my favourites because it made me feel really happy. I made Nan play it all the time. And years later they had it in that film. Lying in bed that night, I could hear it exactly the way it sounded on her old record player. Scratchy and old-fashioned.

"Just blahblah and me … and baby makes three … we're happy in my blue heaven…"

I didn't really understand it when I was little, but I did now. Now I knew what the singer meant.

I drifted off to sleep, softly humming my nan's song. At last I understood what life was all about.

Love Will
Set You Free

Les said I was pretty, fun to be with, and that I made him laugh. I couldn't believe it.

"*Me?*" I'd say.

And he'd say, "Yes, *you.*"

Like me, Les had had a hard time at school. He was quiet, and teachers and other bullies picked on him a lot. Plus, though it was hard to believe *now*, he'd been fat and unpopular. So he was always shy with girls. He said he never even *thought* about girls in secondary school, all he thought about was getting out and getting a job and having a life. Also like me. He only moved out of his mother's and down to London that summer, so though he'd been out with a few girls he'd never even had a real girlfriend. Before now.

"You kiss like you have," I told him.

Les laughed. "Beginner's luck."

Les liked the way boys looked at me in the street, like they wished they were him.

"Green with envy," he'd say as we passed a group of them. "Green with envy." He'd give me a hug. He was really chuffed.

I'd hug him back.

I was really chuffed, too.

Les also liked that I was really feminine and into make-up and stuff. He was a musicals freak. He said I was like some song in some old musical, I enjoyed being a girl.

"I do now," I said.

There were tons of things Les knew about – sports and cars and videos and who originally starred in *Oklahoma!*, that sort of thing – that I didn't know much about. I loved to listen to him explain them to me. And he loved to explain them.

"You're sure I'm not boring you?" he'd ask.

And I'd say, "Of course I'm sure."

But even though we hung out a lot together and were always happy and kissing and stuff, Les never said the L-word. He said he wasn't ready for a serious relationship, but I reckoned he was just shy. I mean, it was all pretty new to him. Les was a boy, so he hadn't spent all the years I'd spent waiting to fall in love. He wasn't prepared. I knew that it can take a man a lot longer to realize he's in love than it does a woman. Like in *When Harry Met Sally...* Though I hoped it wouldn't take him that long.

So I never said the L-word, either. Not that it mattered. I felt it. And I showed it. And I knew that, deep down, Les felt it too.

Besides being ecstatically happy, the beauty of

being in love was that it gave me real power for the first time in my life. Because nothing else mattered. It was that simple. Nothing else mattered at all.

The Wicked Witch of NW6 could moan at me and threaten me and refuse to give me any pocket money, and it didn't matter. I couldn't care less. She was like a toothless, clawless lion roaring at the ringmaster. I might still be living in her flat, but in my mind and heart I was already gone.

It was the same at school. Now there really was no reason why I should worry about boring stuff like science and history. As soon as I was sixteen, I'd leave school, move in with Les and get a job. Les was bound to be a manager by then, and he'd get me something in Blockbuster until we decided it was time to have kids. Before you knew it, I was going to be decorating our flat and making dinner for our friends, not sitting in the library with my nose in a book worrying about who started a war hundreds of years ago. I mean, it wasn't like I was going to have to list the kings and queens of England in chronological order to shop in Sainsbury's, was it?

As usual, the preachers didn't exactly agree with me.

"You're bright enough," Mrs Mela, my English teacher, informed me one afternoon, "but you just don't seem to want to make any effort at all any more."

That's why Mrs Mela had made me stay behind. Because I didn't make any effort *at all* any more.

She'd caught me passing notes to my friend Amie while she was reading us *Romeo and Juliet*. Again.

Thing was, I really didn't want to make any effort just then. I was meeting Les for tea before he went on his shift. Who wants to discuss their lack of interest in English when they've got a date? I stared through the window behind her, as if I was listening and thinking deeply about what she said.

Mrs Mela sighed. She sounded just like Hilary Spiggs.

"Lana," said Mrs Mela in her user-friendly voice, "what's going to happen to you if you keep this up? You haven't done your homework in weeks. You disrupt the rest of the class..." She gave another heartfelt sigh. "I'm very, very concerned."

I flashed her one of my best smiles. "There's nothing to be concerned about," I assured her. "I understand what you're saying, but you're wrong. I'm fine."

Mrs Mela cleared her throat. "And what about your future?" she wanted to know. "What are you going to do with your life? At the rate you're going, you'll be lucky to pass half your GCSEs."

Now she really sounded like my mother.

So I told her the same thing I told my mother and everybody else, so they'd shut up and leave me alone.

"I reckon I'll become an actress. I really like drama."

Actually, acting was the one job I thought would really suit me. You make lots of money, you go to lots of parties and you don't need any qualifications, you just turn up for auditions. What could be easier? You don't even have to go to acting school, if you don't want to. Scads of famous stars were discovered just walking down the street.

"I believe the correct term is 'actor' for both sexes nowadays," said Mrs Mela. "And as far as your love of drama goes, Lana, Shakespeare *is* drama, but you don't seem to like *him* very much."

That's the thing I've always found with preachers, they twist your words to suit themselves.

"I meant like films," I explained. "You know, like *Titanic*. Or musicals." Musicals were starting to interest me a lot. I'd watched at least six since I met Les. "Everyone says I have a really good voice."

"You need more than a good voice to get on in this world," said Mrs Mela. "You need to work hard and get proper qualifications."

Mrs Mela had two university degrees, plus a teaching degree. If I was an underachiever, she was an overachiever. Fancy going to school for twenty years just to teach English to a load of kids who'd rather be at home watching telly.

I readjusted my school bag over my shoulder. "So, is that all?" I prepared for flight. "It's just that I have to get home. My mum's got the flu."

I got the feeling from the way Mrs Mela frowned at me that my mum had had the flu before. Probably recently.

"How old are you?" asked Mrs Mela. "Fifteen?"

You didn't need a university degree to guess that, either. I was in Year Ten, wasn't I?

I nodded.

"Fifteen's old enough to start taking things seriously," said Mrs Mela. She smiled hopefully. "With a little effort on your part, this year could see your attitude mature a little more."

"I'll try," I lied. "I'm sure it will."

I couldn't see how much more mature she expected my attitude to get. Only one more year and I'd be out of school for good.

My best friend, Shanee Tyler, was the complete opposite of me.

Shanee was small, dark, quiet and plain as a wholemeal digestive. I was into fashion, but Shanee couldn't tell DKNY from CK. Plus, her mum had three kids and no husband, so they were always broke. Most of the time, she dressed in old jeans, and she didn't even own a pair of trainers, never mind platforms or heels. She wore hiking boots and somebody's hand-me-down motorcycle boots that looked like something out of *Star Wars*. And forget make-up. The only time she let me do her up, she'd moaned and moved so much that I nearly put her eye out. And, unlike me, Shanee was polite, well-behaved, worked hard and was good at school. The perfect daughter.

But even though we were so different, Shanee

and I had been best friends since primary school.

She was waiting for me in the hall when Mrs Mela finally let me go.

"I saw you through the door," said Shanee. "What'd she want?"

I shrugged. "Oh, you know…" Shanee didn't *really* know. She never got in trouble. "She caught me passing notes with Amie, and then I didn't know what page we were on in the stupid play and then it turned out that I didn't have my homework—"

"*Turned out*?" Shanee smirked. "What do you mean it *turned out* that you didn't have your homework?"

I gave her a look. "I forgot it."

She spluttered. "You mean you forgot to do it."

Shanee knew me too well.

"More or less." I grinned. "Old mealy-mouth went mad. So I had to hear the lecture about making an effort and thinking about the future and all that stuff."

Shanee adjusted her school bag on her shoulder.

"You'd think she'd get tired of saying it," said Shanee.

I laughed. "Preachers are robots. They just repeat the same things over and over."

Shanee kicked a drinks can out of her path. "On the other hand, I suppose you have let your usual low standards drop a bit lately…"

If my mother had made a crack like that, it would've been a criticism, but with Shanee I knew she was just joking.

"You know," she went on, "you used to do your homework now and then." She gave me a smile. "Or at least copy someone else's."

"I couldn't copy someone else's English, it was an essay. Plus, Amie's useless at English and she's the only one who would let me."

Shanee laughed. "You really are too much sometimes..."

I was laughing, too. We stepped through the gates.

"I've got a life now, Shanee. I'm not going to waste my time trying to work out what some dead geezer wrote hundreds of years ago. It's not redolent."

"You mean *relevant*," said Shanee. "Redolent has to do with smell."

I flapped one hand. "Whatever you say."

She stopped just outside the gates and looked at me with her head to one side.

"Where are you going?" she demanded. "The garden centre's left."

I was going right, towards the café.

"Oh, didn't I tell you? I'm meeting Les for tea before he goes to work."

Shanee's mouth formed a perfect O.

"What about our science project?"

We were working in pairs. Shanee and I were finding out about the effects of light and water on plants. This was the day we were meant to buy our seeds.

"You don't need me to pick out a packet of seeds."

Shanee was quiet, but she was stubborn.

"What about planting them?" she insisted. "Do you expect me to do it all on my own?"

"I trust you," I assured her. "I'm sure you'll do a brilliant job."

Shanee rolled her eyes. "Don't tell me," she said. "Who needs photosynthesis when they've got love?"

I forgot all about Mrs Mela and Shanee for the rest of the afternoon. I had a great time.

After tea, I walked Les to work. The other guy on the night shift hadn't turned up yet, so I helped out behind the counter till he did. You had to log in each title that was being taken in or out on the computer. I'd done pretty well in my computer class, so I had no trouble. Les was impressed.

"It took me ages just to learn how to call up a file." He gave me a quick kiss. "Not only pretty but clever, too."

No one had ever called me clever before.

Later, he came up behind me while I was putting some titles back on the shelves and gave me a squeeze.

"*And* she's a hard worker," he informed an invisible audience. "What more could one man ask?"

I laughed. Mrs Mela and Hilary Spiggs would've had heart attacks if they'd heard Les describe me as "a hard worker". But that was the whole point, wasn't it? I was a hard worker when there was some reason to be one. Plus, I liked working in the video shop. It made me feel grown up and in charge. And responsible, just like everyone was always telling me I should be.

I was about to kiss Les back, but at that moment someone came into the shop. He pushed me away.

"No fraternizing on company time," he whispered, giving me another squeeze.

A thrill ran through me. It was like having a secret no one else knew. How grown up could you get?

The other guy didn't show up till nearly six, so by the time he was settled, and Les and I had said goodbye, and I'd walked home, it was after seven.

She was in the kitchen, drinking a beer and making a curry.

She turned as I reached the doorway.

"Where've you been?"

"Out."

I hadn't told *her* about Les, of course. It was my private, personal life and had nothing to do with her. She'd only try to ruin it for me. Plus, she'd probably want to meet him, you know, check his teeth and his intentions and stuff like that. The mind boggled. Even if Les didn't get scared that I was going to turn into an old bag with dyed hair and the dress sense of a tramp – and even if she didn't tell him how old I really was straight away – she'd be sure to tell him enough of my faults to put him off for good. I could just hear her. "Did you know she cuts her toenails over the living-room carpet? Have you seen the state of her room? She's violent, you know. She threw the remote control through the front window last winter because I told her to do her homework…" That's what she was like. Moan, moan, moan. Worse, though, was the fact that if she knew I had a boyfriend who came round after work on the nights she went to Charley's, she'd stay at home. I knew her. She was mean. Anything to spoil my fun.

She put down the knife she'd been chopping carrots with.

"Out where?"

I threw my bag on the table and draped my jacket over a chair. "Doing my science project with Shanee. How long till we eat?"

She gave me her mind-reading stare.

"I had a call from Mrs Mela."

She said it like it was some kind of threat. Which I suppose it was.

I took an apple from the fruit bowl. "Have I got time for a shower?"

She leaned against the counter, her arms folded in front of her in typical telling-off mode.

"She says your work is slipping."

I bit into the apple. "Shakespeare's boring. I

don't understand it."

I could see the tip of her tongue between her lips.

"That's why you're doing Shakespeare at school. So someone can tell you what it means."

"Yeah ... right..." I took another bite. "Well, I am doing it at school, aren't I?"

"Apparently not," said Hilary Spiggs. "Apparently you're writing notes and making jokes at school."

I started to ease back out of the kitchen. "I'm going to have a shower before sup—"

"You're going to stay right here and tell me what's going on."

I met her eyes, my face expressionless. "Nothing's going on. I don't like Shakespeare."

"Mrs Mela says it's not just her class."

"Well, she's wrong."

Old stone-face didn't even blink.

"Something's going on," she informed me. "Ever since your birthday you've been acting oddly." She narrowed her eyes into two dark, probing slits. "Are you seeing someone, Lana? Is that what it is?"

I didn't think my mother was the *stupidest* person on the planet, but I definitely thought she was one of them. I mean, she knew nothing about life or love or anything like that. And if she'd ever been younger than thirty she'd blocked it out completely. But sometimes she surprised me. Like now. How could she *tell*?

"Of course I'm seeing someone." I smiled very

43

sweetly. It drove her mad. "I see dozens of people a day. Shanee, Amie, Gerri, Meryl, Lisa—"

"Please," said the Grand Inquisitor. "Spare me the list. You know what I mean. Are you seeing someone? A boy?"

I tossed my apple core into the bin. "It'd be pretty hard *not* to see a few hundred of them. It's a mixed school, remember?"

She picked up her beer. "Yes," she said. "I do remember."

Not Quite
Romeo and Juliet

"So how's your science project going?" Annie asked one lunch-break.

Shanee squashed her drink carton under her foot.

"OK. My plants seem to be doing what they're meant to be doing. You know, different stuff depending on how much light and water they get ... I haven't lost any yet." She looked over at me. "What about yours, Lana?"

I groaned. "Oh, my God, the plants..."

Shanee bought the seeds, planted the seeds, separated the tiny plants out into pots, and then gave me a dozen to look after. I was meant to put three in a place where they got a lot of light, three in a place where they got a bit of light, three in a place where they didn't get much light, and the rest in the dark. I was meant to check them every day and keep notes. I was meant to be making scientific observations.

"I totally forgot about them … I've been so busy lately…"

"Not doing homework obviously," said Gerri.

Shanee bit back a smile.

"No," said Amie in this baby voice. "With *Les*…" She gave me one of her sour looks. "I thought he had a job. Doesn't he ever go to it?"

"You know, you're not the only one with a boyfriend, Lana," purred Gerri. "Other people manage to have a love life *and* occasionally get some work done."

It was as if their bodies had been taken over not by aliens but by preachers. What was wrong with everyone all of a sudden?

"I never said I was the only one with a boyfriend," I snapped back. "I just said I've been busy."

Amie snorted. "Yeah, right."

"So what'd you do last night?" asked Shanee, the Peacemaker. "Anything exciting?"

The other two spluttered.

"Nothing special. The old bag went to Charley's, so Les came over after work and we hung out."

The first couple of weeks we were going out, Les and me did do things. We went to the park and had tea in the café; we went to the cinema; we had a meal in the pizza place by the station; he took me for a drive up to Hendon because he loved roundabouts. But as time went on, *nothing special* was all we did. Not that I was complaining. I wasn't complaining. I'd be happy watching paint dry with Les. Doing *nothing* with Les was a hundred times better than doing *something* with anybody else. I'd meet him for tea after school, or I'd drop by the shop, and, if Hilary was out, he'd come round at about eleven-thirty or twelve, after he finished work and the pubs had closed. We'd watch a bit of telly, then we'd snog for a while, and then he'd go home. He never invited me round to his, because he lived with four other guys and there wasn't any privacy. He wanted me all to himself.

Gerri glanced over at me. "Have you slept with him yet?"

Gerri'd been having sex since the day before her fourteenth birthday. So, since she was thirteen. At least that's what she said. She never actually went into much detail.

"No, not yet." I crumbled up my sandwich wrapper. "Les is a gentleman. He never pressures me."

This was true, but it did puzzle me a bit. Boys were *meant* to want sex; they were meant to pressure you. But Les never did. We'd snog in his car, we'd snog in my flat when Hilary was out, we'd even snogged in the Blockbuster office a couple of times, but he never tried to go any further. Most of the time I didn't think about it, but when I *did* think about it I couldn't decide if there was something wrong with Les, or with me.

I wasn't the only one.

"Oh, *puhlease*..." Amie spluttered with laughter.

47

"Are you sure there's nothing wrong with him?"

"Maybe he's gay," said Gerri. "Only he doesn't know it yet."

I'd seen that film, too. Only the guy Kevin Kline played was obviously gay. I mean, it was incredible that it'd never occurred to him or anyone else. Les wasn't anything like that.

Shanee waded in again.

"Maybe they have a real relationship," said Shanee. "It doesn't mean a person's gay just because he's interested in more than sex. "

"Exactly." I could always count on Shanee. "Not every boy is sex-mad, you know."

"Wanting to have sex with your girlfriend isn't being sex-mad," Amie shot back. "It's natural."

Gerri's smile was as slimy as a slug trail. "You have been seeing Les for a while now. You'd think he'd at least ask."

I raised one eyebrow. "And how do you know he hasn't?"

Amie burst out laughing. "Oh, I get it," she said. "It's not Les who's gay. It's *you*."

Personally, I think life would be a lot easier if it came with instructions. You know, like a video or a stereo system. So you wouldn't always have to be wondering what was going on and what you were supposed to do about it.

I'd always found magazines very helpful like that, so I went straight home after school and looked through every women's magazine I had. There were stacks of them, because my mother was always going to take them to the recycling but never did. I reckoned one of them was bound to have something that dealt with my problem. If not a feature, then a letter:

Dear Auntie, My boyfriend and I have been going out for a year now, and he's never tried to have sex with me. People say I'm pretty. What's wrong?

There wasn't much. There was a lot on clothes and make-up and exercise and how men are different to women (in case you hadn't noticed) and stuff like that, but not anything that was exactly like my problem.

There was a letter in *Cosmo*, or maybe *Marie Claire*, from a woman whose husband never wanted to have sex with her any more. It had been four months. He always said he was tired or stressed out from work. The agony aunt said that the husband *was* probably tired and stressed out from work. She said that women had the idea that all men wanted to have sex *all* the time, but that this wasn't true. Men were people, too. Sometimes they felt like having sex, and sometimes they didn't. If you'd had a hard day at work, she said, you weren't going to feel like breaking the bedsprings when you got home, and men didn't either.

Even though I didn't learn anything very helpful from the magazines, I felt better knowing that men really weren't meant to be horny all the time. It took off quite a bit of pressure. I mean, it definitely wasn't him *or* me, was it? It was just life.

And then I remembered a film I saw once. It was about a man and woman who lived together, but just as flatmates. They became really good friends, but he never made a pass at her or *anything*. She couldn't work out why. But it was because he knew she'd been raped once and was nervous of sex. That's why he'd decided they would just be friends, because he loved her and didn't want to lose her completely. When she finds out the truth, she seduces him and everything's OK.

It wasn't exactly like me and Les, but it was close enough. Les didn't know I was only fifteen, but he knew I'd never had a boyfriend. He was probably just being sensitive and tactful. He was a very sensitive and tactful person. He didn't want to take advantage.

It was two nights after the conversation with Amie, Shanee and Gerri before I saw Les again. He rang up on Friday to say he was coming round, but that somebody at work was getting married and they were going for a drink to celebrate, so he'd be a bit later than usual. I'd been pretty certain he would come round. Hilary almost always went to Charley's on a Friday night.

By then I had made my plan. I reckoned it was time. I mean, since I already knew I was going to marry Les and have his babies I couldn't see any reason for holding back. The sooner we started, the sooner I'd get away from Hilary Spiggs.

But *I* wasn't going to seduce *him*. I didn't think

I was up to seducing someone yet. It'd be like taking a job as a manicurist when you'd never even had your nails done yourself. Plus, since Les wasn't exactly experienced with girls, I reckoned he might not be up to it either. Maybe he needed some encouragement. All the magazines agreed that men were not as confident about sex as they seemed to be. Especially someone as sensitive as Les. So I was going to make it possible for him to seduce me without wondering whether or not he was going to be rejected.

As soon as my mother left, I had a bath. I put in three bath pearls and played a George Michael album to get me in a sexy mood. I lay there, using my toes to turn on the hot tap to top up the water, imagining Les seducing me.

"Let me give you a back rub," he'd whisper. "Let me just see you naked, I swear I won't do anything."

I, of course, was all coy and shy.

"Oh, I don't know ... what if someone comes ... I feel so embarrassed..."

Les was quiet and gentle.

"Don't be," Les said softly. "I'll help you undress ... I'll stop whenever you say..."

I got as far as him sliding his hand behind me to undo my bra, but then I stopped. I didn't want to ruin the best part for myself.

After my bath, I spent a couple of hours getting dressed and made-up. I wanted to be provocative, but subtle. Which meant I had to wear something that would have the effect of a miniskirt and stilettos, but that wasn't so obvious. In the end, I found inspiration in the cinema, as per usual. I wore my tartan boxer shorts and bra, with one of Charley's white shirts over it. I think it was Ellen Barkin I saw dressed like that, and it was incredibly sexy.

I borrowed some of Hilary's Opium that she bought when Charley took us to Disney World. It was old, but it smelled OK, and she had tons of it left because she only wore it for very special occasions and she didn't have many of those. While I was in her room I also borrowed her large gold hoop earrings and her thinnest gold chain. Ellen Barkin always wore gold, and our hair colour was almost exactly the same. At least sometimes.

It was just as well I *knew* Les was going to be late, because after *I* was ready, it took me ages to get my bedroom ready.

The first thing I did was take Mr Ted, my teddy from when I was little, off the bed. I'd never spent a night without Mr Ted that I could remember, but I didn't think a stuffed bear was really appropriate in a seduction scene. Plus, it would've been strange fooling around with Mr Ted sitting there with his one eye. I put him on my shelf, facing the wall.

Then I went through the whole flat and got every candle I could find: night-lights, Christmas candles, garden candles, the big candles in glass jars with saints painted on them that Charley brought back from Florida, the candles the two of them had in the kitchen for when they went camping, the beeswax candles I made in primary school that Hilary never bothered using, even the special round candle that looked like stained glass when it burned that Charlene gave me. In films, someone's always filling a room with dozens and dozens of burning candles. I wanted my room to look like that. Candles are really romantic. I don't know who lights all those candles in the films, but I bet it's more than one person. I didn't have more than twenty candles, but it took me *hours* to get them all going. I'd light two or three, and the first one would go out. Or I'd get six going on my chest of drawers, and half of them would be blown out when I walked past. By the time they were all lit, the room looked like there'd been a gunfight in it and the first few candles had gone out again.

I was spraying a little more Opium into the room, to get rid of the smell of sulphur from all the matches, when the doorbell rang.

I raced into the hall, took a deep breath, and smiled.

"Hello, babe."

Les leaned over me from the doorway. His gaze was like a sponge sucking up spilled lotion. "Is that a bikini under that shirt?"

He had the glazed eyes and fixed smile of a man watching a dancer in a topless bar. I could feel myself flush. God bless you, Ellen Barkin!

"Sort of."

Half of me wanted the neighbours to see me getting off with him on the doorstep, but the other half of me knew that if they did, one of them would blab to Her Majesty sooner or later.

I gave Les a tug to pull him inside, and he sort of tripped past me.

I tossed my head so he could see my earrings. Dangly earrings are *very* sexy.

"You look like you had a good time," I teased.

Les propped himself against the entrance to the living room, grinning like a Hallowe'en pumpkin.

"Videos," he mumbled. "We watched these videos…" The pumpkin smile turned into a leer. "It would've been better if you'd been there."

My blood began to bubble. Les had never *leered* at me before.

"Really?" I purred. "Are you *sure*?"

Les swallowed and sort of sucked on his lips. His head bobbed up and down.

"You look good." He held out his arms. "You gonna give me a kiss?"

I moistened my lips and started walking towards him, slowly. "*Maybe…*"

The "*maybe*" always works.

He lurched forwards, pinning me against the wall. He was bigger than me. I was powerless beneath his weight. It was pretty exciting. His breath smelled like the kitchen after one of my mother's parties, but it was masculine and almost intoxicating. Unless I was just getting drunk on the fumes.

54

"I'll kiss you till Peter Pan grows up..." I whispered.

It was a line from a film, but Les didn't recognize it.

"You should be a writer." His lips touched mine. "Or a professional kisser..."

I couldn't believe it! We'd been seeing each other for over six weeks and I'd never even got my bra all the way off. But all of a sudden he was all over me. Tongue, hands, knee, even face. He kept rubbing his cheek against mine, which was like being licked by a very large and strong cat. I ignored the slight pain and rubbed back. The last person in the world I wanted to see right then (or ever, really) was Hilary Spiggs, but in a weird way I wanted her to see *me*. There's your little girl, Mrs Spiggs, put that in your teacup and drink it!

"Let's go to bed."

I was speaking softly, the way you do in romantic moments, and my face was squashed against his neck, so I wasn't sure he heard me. I gave him a shove.

"It's late ... let's go to my room..."

It never occurred to me that it would be so easy.

"Bed," said Les, and he kind of tottered backwards.

I grabbed hold of him and steered him down the hallway.

I reached round him and opened the door to my room. I suppose he didn't realize, because he lurched forward, pulling me with him. He straightened up immediately, and I bounced against the door.

"Jesus Christ!" I'd never heard Les sound frightened before. "The place is on fire!"

For a second I thought it really was on fire. I'd forgotten all about the candles. Fire was a definite possibility.

I looked round him, and started breathing again with relief.

"It's all right," I assured him. Nothing was burning that shouldn't have been. "It's just the candles."

He nodded, slowly, like I'd explained something very complicated to him and he was taking it in.

"Oh, right. The candles."

I'd half thought he might scoop me up in his arms the way Nicolas Cage scoops up Cher in *Moonstruck*, but I suppose to be fair to Les he was having enough trouble holding himself up, without holding me up, too.

He grabbed hold of me, and started licking at my ear. It sort of reminded me of Nan's dog.

"You light my candle," Les murmured.

"Me too," I murmured back. "I've never felt like this before."

Les burped. "Me neither." He ran his hand over my breasts. "I've never felt you like this before either."

Things got a little hectic after that. I'd never seen him so worked up. And because he was so excited, I was excited, too. Scenes of passion flashed before my eyes. Some were even in black and white.

Kissing and sort of climbing all over each other, we finally reached the bed. I helped him get out of his shoes and trousers. I had to leave him for a second, to turn the stereo on, and when I got back he was stretched out with a smile on his face.

"Baby..." he moaned. "Baby ... baby..."

"Les..." I whispered. "Les, get under the duvet."

I climbed in beside him.

His eyes were closed, but he immediately wrapped himself around me and nuzzled close. His leg rubbed against mine.

"Skin..." mumbled Les, yanking at my bra. "Skin on skin..."

Skin on skin...

It was the most grown-up thing anyone'd ever said to me. I kissed him with passion. He kissed me back.

Over and over.

We were kissing and groaning and all that stuff, and then Les started pushing against me. I could feel him sort of groping around between us.

Push ... push ... grunt ... grunt...

"I can't find it," gasped Les.

I wasn't sure what he was looking for.

Push ... push ... grunt ... grunt...

And then there was this little jolt of pain and Les's eyes moved around like he was having some sort of fit, and then he rolled on to his back.

"Geez," he panted. "Was that your first time, too?"

This is going to sound weird, but I didn't really know it'd happened until then. First of all, I didn't remember him putting on a condom. I wasn't sure, but I had the impression it wasn't something you could do too far in advance. Plus, it wasn't exactly how I'd imagined.

I propped myself on one elbow and leaned against his chest. "You mean you've never done it before, either?"

Les was staring at the ceiling. He shook his head. "What'd you think?" he asked.

I kissed the side of his head. "What did *you* think?"

He grinned. "I thought it was great."

I nestled my head on his shoulder.

"So did I."

Earth Calling
Lana Spiggs

When I look back at it now, I reckon sleeping with Les must have put me in some kind of trance. Like a fairy tale, but in reverse. Instead of the Prince's kiss waking me up, it put me to sleep.

Everything sloshed around me in a blur. I went through the motions of eating and sleeping and watching telly and carrying my books back and forth to school, but without really connecting any of those activities to my brain. All I could think of was our future. Mine and Les's. The Emerald City of Oz had nothing on that.

It took me a long time to get anywhere, because I was always stopping to look at something. I read the notices in estate agents' windows, looking for the perfect flat for me and Les. I stopped at every furniture shop I passed (except the second-hand ones) to check out what they had. I even went out of my way to go past places that sold prams and stuff like that. Plus, I read all my mother's catalogues, especially the ones from Argos and Ikea, from cover to cover, dozens of times. I picked out the pots and pans and bath towels Les and I would have. I picked out the furniture and the curtains. I imagined having people round and them admiring what we'd done with the flat.

"Lana did it all," Les would say proudly. "She's the perfect wife."

I was happy.

I was finally a woman; why shouldn't I be happy?

Not that everything was all rosy, cosy. My nan always said there were flies in every ointment, and there were definitely flies in the ointment of my love.

The biggest flies were my mother and her boy-friend. Hilary and Charley always had a big fight before Christmas, when they broke up once and for all. They'd been together for six years, and for six years they'd been breaking up forever at Christ-- mas.

"This is it!" she'd shriek. "I never want to see him again!"

And she'd take all the presents he'd given her (except things like the telly and the stereo, of course) and put them in a box and leave it in the hall for him to collect. He never bothered. They usually made up in time to go out for New Year's Eve.

This year was just like the ones before. On

the tenth of December (a little earlier than usual) my mother announced that she and Charley had broken up for good, and asked if I wanted to go to the cinema with her that night.

The row between my mum and Charley really messed up my new love life. Since Hilary hardly ever went out unless she dragged me with her, Les couldn't drop round any more. And I couldn't come and go as I pleased, either – not without making up some place to be going and someone who wasn't Les to go there with. Without Charley to occupy her, she watched me like a hawk.

I was just getting used to all that when Christmas itself came. Les was going up to Norwich for a week to see his mother. He took me to his house for the first time the night before he went away. There was no one else at home, since they'd all gone away for the holidays. At least we'd have a chance to do it again.

Les's house looked like all the other houses on the road, comfortable family houses, a bit on the posh side. There weren't any council flats on Les's street.

Inside, though, it was different because there wasn't even a living-room, just five bedrooms and a kitchen. The only room I saw beside Les's was the kitchen. It was incredibly tidy for five guys living alone, but Les was a very tidy person. Even when he made us tea, he washed the spoon and put it in the drainer before we took our cups upstairs.

Les's room was the smallest. It had a telly and a

mattress on the floor and a computer.

"Well?" asked Les. "What do you think?"

It was tidy and everything, but it was kind of bare. I could see it needed a woman's touch.

"It's nice," I said. "But it could do with a couple of pictures. You know, to make it look more cosy."

He grinned at me affectionately. "I'd never have thought of that."

I gave Les a really gorgeous jumper from Covent Garden. He reminded me of Kevin Costner in it. It cost so much I had to give everybody else chocolates.

Les gave me a gold charm bracelet from Argos. It had one charm, a tiny hamburger, plated in gold.

"It reminded me of you," said Les. "Do you like it?"

It wasn't a gold heart, but I definitely liked it.

"I love it!" I cried. "It's the best present I've ever had." I hugged him hard.

But that was the only thing that did get hard that night.

We rolled around on his single mattress, banging our knees against the wall and whacking each other with elbows, but nothing happened except we knocked over the teas.

Les apologized. He said it was because he lived with so many other people. It made him self-conscious. Even though they were away he was expecting one of them to burst into the room at any minute. That's what his flatmates were like.

I took it in my stride. This sort of thing was always happening on TV.

"It's OK," I assured him. "It happens to everyone."

"You're wonderful," said Les. He kissed my forehead. "And very mature for eighteen."

Maybe I wouldn't've been so mature if I'd known it was going to be our last chance to be together for weeks and weeks.

I'd always liked Christmas, especially when I was little, but that year it was a drag. Everybody went to Charlene's, as per usual, since she had the kids. And, also as per usual, Nan ended up doing most of the cooking while her daughter and grand-daughters (with one glaring exception, of course) all got sloshed. Every year Dara made us sit through the entire Phil Spector Christmas album at least a dozen times, and every year everyone begged her not to. Hilary spent about eight hours in the kitchen, crying about Charley. Every time I opened the door because I'd been sent to get something she was saying the same thing. "This is really it ... this time there won't be a next time..." and slobbering into her wine. Only she was always saying it to someone different – Charlene, Dara, Charlene's boyfriend, Justin, Dara's boyfriend, Mick, Nan, even Drew and Courtney, Charlene's kids... Once, I actually caught her telling the fridge. Charlene's boyfriend and Dara's boyfriend got into a fight about football. Charlene and Dara got into a fight over whether or not Charlene's children watched too much telly. Charlene's kids were always fighting. I tried to ignore them all by pretending that I wasn't really there.

I pretended I was at home with Les. He'd left his mum's straight after dinner to surprise me. I'd come home on my own from Charlene's and there he was, waiting for me. He'd bought an artificial silver tree and decorated it with red balls and tiny green lights that looked like wreaths, just like the one I saw in Paperchase. There were about a million presents under it, and they were all wrapped in shiny paper, not the cheap stuff Hilary bought in the market, ten rolls for a quid, and half of them said Happy Birthday or For Your Wedding Anniversary. These were really beautiful and elegant, and they were all tied with real satin ribbons not those plasticky stick-on bows favoured by doctors' receptionists. Me and Les sipped champagne while we opened our presents. Les was just trying on one of the presents I'd given him – a silk Armani jacket – when I realized that my nan was shouting at me. It was hard to hear her because the telly *and* the stereo were blaring, and, besides everybody talking and the kids shrieking, Charlene and Hilary were arguing now.

I blinked. "What?"

Nan knocked back her sherry.

"You're very quiet today. You coming down with something?"

If only I was. Then maybe someone would drive

me home and I really would find that Les had left his mother and was waiting for me. At least I'd have some peace and quiet so I could think about him.

"It's because I'm practically an adult," I informed her. "Your daughter doesn't realize it, but I'm not a child any more."

"I'm glad to hear it," said my nan. "Then you can be in charge of the washing-up."

Not only did Les not come home early, but he got sick the day after Boxing Day and couldn't come home at all.

"You're joking," I said. "What have you got, the plague?"

"Flu," croaked Les. "The doctor says it could take a couple of weeks. Maybe more."

"God…" For me, two or three weeks without Les was like two or three weeks without water. Plus, I'd read of people dying from the flu. "Maybe you should come back to London. I could come over and nurse you."

Les sighed with pain and fever. His voice was low and strained.

"My mother wouldn't hear of it," he said. "Besides, I've got the car. There's no way I could drive."

I asked him for his mother's number, so I could ring him when she was out.

"She won't let me out of bed to talk on the phone," said Les. "I'm only ringing now because she's gone into town. And if she knew I was making a long-distance call on her phone... She's on a fixed income, you know. She counts every penny."

"Well, give me the address then." I'd write to him every day. Letters and postcards. Little presents to cheer him up.

"Oh, no," said Les. "My mum's back. I'll ring you again if I can."

After that call, I talked to Les in my head all the time. I stayed in my room, listening out for the phone, writing him letters and notes that I planned to send when he rang back with the address.

Dear Les, I don't know how to say this, but I really love you. I love everything about you. Even when you get angry...

Dear Les, Today I had breakfast (toast and cereal and two cups of tea) and went out to the shops, but all I could think of was you...

Dear Les, I hope you're getting plenty of rest and eating the right foods. You should drink plenty of liquids...

But he never rang back. His mother must've been watching him like a hawk.

Either that or he'd died.

Les didn't die, but he also didn't come back to London for three weeks. The longest three weeks of my life. I'd forgotten how boring and empty my life had been without him, but it all came back pretty quickly. Some days I felt like he'd never existed. The dumb, dull days stretched into dumb, dull nights. I ate, I slept, I watched TV. I was like a hamster going round and round in its wheel. The same things to do, the same arguments, the same big nothing.

Even the Spiggs noticed how depressed I was.

"It's not like you to look like that in the holidays," she said over supper one night.

"Like what?" I asked, thinking of words like "tragic" and "heartbroken" and "stricken with grief".

"Like you've got a life sentence with hard labour," said my mother.

I gave her a meaningful look. "I have."

Les got back on a Friday. He rang me as soon as he walked through his front door.

Hilary and Charley still hadn't made up. She was only a few feet away in the kitchen, descaling the kettle, her ears up like a hunting dog's.

I turned my back on her.

"Oh, Amie," I said, in a bright, casual voice. "What's up?"

"Amie?" said Les. "Lana, it's me. Les. I just got back."

"Oh, you poor thing…" I said. "Are you feeling better now?"

"Oh, I get it," said Les. "You can't talk. Yeah, I'm still weak, but I'm much better." He lowered his voice. "I've been thinking about you."

Fudge sauce flowed through my veins.

"Me, too," I said. "A lot…" I smiled into the receiver. "Maybe we can go to a film or something. Now that you're better."

"Not tonight," my mother shouted. "You're going shopping with me. Remember?"

How could I forget something as exciting as that?

"I'll have to see what's happening," said Les. "I've been off work a while."

It was times like these that convinced me that once I'd had my family, I was going to have a great career as an actress. There wasn't a shred of disappointment in my voice as I said, "Oh, of course. I know you've got a lot to catch up on."

"And I missed all the holiday parties," said Les. "I've got some people to see."

I almost said, "And what am I? Sliced bread?" but I didn't have to. Les, as per usual, knew how I felt.

"Tell you what," said Les. "Why don't you come round to the shop tomorrow? I'm on nights."

"All right," I said. "I'll see you then."

"And wear those boxer shorts you wore that time," said Les. He laughed. "Just so I know."

I smiled, drowning in fudge sauce. He really had been thinking of me.

The winter slogged on, dull and grey. My life was pretty dull and grey, too. Hilary was usually at home in the evenings and Les was usually working. Because Shanee lived with her mother, her two little brothers, her one little sister (who shared a room with her), two cats, a dog and an assortment of other small mammals – and had less privacy than a traffic light – she'd come to mine more than I'd gone to hers since we started secondary school, but now that changed.

With the ointment of my love clogged with dead flies, I had nowhere else to go. I wasn't seeing much of Les because he was so busy and Hilary had cemented herself to the couch. The Tylers' was like a madhouse with all the keepers on their tea break, but it was better than solitary confinement with a prison guard who never stopped nagging you about your homework and how much make-up you were wearing and where you were going and when you were coming back and who you were going to see.

"God…" I shouted over the noise from the television, Shanee's brothers and the radio that was blaring from her bedroom. "I really miss it sometimes, you know?"

I looked over. Shanee had her eyes on the film we were watching. Her brothers were sitting on the floor in front of us, impersonating an air strike and throwing crayons at each other.

"You really should try it," I went on. "It's so *cool.*"

Shanee nodded. "I know," she said, still watching Robert De Niro and Sharon Stone snogging passionately. "I intend to try it. Eventually."

I hugged myself. "Sex…" I sighed longingly. "There's nothing like it."

To tell the truth, I kind of enjoyed talking about sex with Les more than I'd actually enjoyed doing it. I mean, it was all right – it was great – but it wasn't the big deal everyone made out. The kissing and stroking was nice, but it didn't last that long, and the deed itself was over almost as soon as it began. I'd nicked a couple of sex manuals from the library, so I knew that these things can take time. Practice makes perfect. If you have anywhere to practise – which we didn't.

Shanee clicked the remote control and got to her feet.

"I'm going to get something to drink," she announced. "Anybody else want anything?"

They *all* wanted something, including the dog.

I followed Shanee into the kitchen, still discussing sex, the way women do.

In many ways, she was the perfect audience, since she had no personal experience whatsoever and I could tell her anything I liked without worrying that she'd know better. The closest Shanee'd ever got to a boy was when one bumped into her on the street.

Shanee opened the fridge and looked inside.

"So, when are you seeing Les again?" she asked, cutting me off in mid-sentence.

"I saw him yesterday." I took five glasses from the draining-board. I'd seen Les at work again, but it was a busy night and I didn't stay long. "But not, you know, *intimately*."

"So I gathered."

The disadvantage of Shanee as an audience was that, having no personal experience, her interest wore off pretty fast.

"It'd be a lot better if you had a boyfriend, too," I complained. "Then you'd want to talk about sex. This is like trying to describe Miami to someone who's never left the Hebrides."

Shanee re-emerged from the fridge with two cartons of juice. "Miami and Disney World aren't the same thing," she informed me.

I stared back at her. I had no idea what she meant.

Shanee sighed. "So how long has it been?" she asked.

We'd only ever really done it once but Shanee didn't need to know that. We had tried a few times but something always seemed to go wrong. The first time was when the Wicked Witch went to Hastings to see my nan. But we were so excited to have the flat to ourselves that we finished off her Christmas port *and* the sherry. Most of what I remembered involved throwing up in my waste-paper basket in the middle of the night. The only other times we'd tried were in the back of his car and once in the shop after it was closed. It was too cold in the car to actually take any clothes off, which was just as well since we'd just got into a serious clinch when a police car pulled up beside us. And I couldn't undress in the shop, all those videos made it hard to get in the mood.

"A week," I lied. "A whole, excruciating week."

Shanee nodded towards the cupboard over the sink. "There's crisps and biscuits up in there," she directed.

I reached for the snacks. "I don't know how much longer I can last," I confessed. "I really miss him."

"My mum hasn't had a boyfriend since my dad left five years ago," said Shanee. "She doesn't seem to mind."

"That's 'cause she's old. It's different when you're in your prime."

Shanee started filling the glasses with juice. "Physical exercise," she decided. "You should take up cross-country running or some—"

I looked over at her. She was staring at me with her head to one side, as though she'd just noticed I had four arms or something.

"What?"

Shanee gave herself a shake. "Nothing." She turned back to the glasses. "I was just wondering if those were the jeans you got at Brent Cross with me in September?"

I put the biscuits and the crisps on the counter. "Yeah. Why?"

She shrugged. "I dunno. They look different."

I tugged at the waist. "They shrunk," I told her. "*She* can't even wash a pair of jeans without ruining them."

"That must be it..." She glanced over and smirked. "Or did you hit the Christmas goodies a little hard?"

"God, no! I hardly ate the whole time. I was lovesick, remember?"

Shanee was still studying me like I was one of her

science project plants. "Your face looks fatter."

I picked up the crisps and two of the glasses.

"It's all the kissing," I assured her. "The muscles swell."

I didn't feel like sitting with my mother the moaner, so I spent most of that night in my room, pretending to be doing my homework while I listened to the radio and imagined me and Les going away together on holiday in the spring, to celebrate our six-month anniversary. To Ibiza, or Greece, somewhere hot and romantic. We found a secluded cove where no one else ever went. The water was as blue as a swimming-pool and the sand was as soft as feathers and as white as Nivea. We put our blanket near the water. I unhooked my bikini top and lay on my front while Les knelt over me, rubbing sunblock into my back.

But I couldn't fall asleep. Every time I closed my eyes and tried to stop thinking about our holiday, I'd see Shanee looking at me with her head to one side, telling me my face was fat.

As soon as I heard Hilary snoring next door, I crept into the living-room to watch telly. I didn't like lying in the dark on my own. It made me nervous. I'm a person who likes light and noise.

There was a pretty funny film on Channel Five. Funny enough to take my mind off my fat face for a while. Normally, I get something to eat or drink while the ads are on, but after what Shanee said I didn't dare go near the kitchen in case I really was gaining weight. I was sitting there, humming along with the jingles the way you do, when the Tampax ad came on. This girl all in white was running around in the sunshine.

Yeah, right, I thought. Like she never leaks even a little...

And that's when it occurred to me that I hadn't had my period yet that month. I tried to shove the thought away, but it kept coming back.

I know it sounds mad that I had no idea when I'd last had one, but it isn't that mad. It wasn't always regular. Sometimes it was late, or I missed a month if I was dieting or if *she* was giving me a really hard time. It'd never bothered me if it didn't come when it should. But then it could never've meant that I was pregnant before.

I was still sitting there, staring at the screen, thinking about the last time I'd had my period when the film came on again.

Not this month so far. Not in January. Not in December.

That can't be right, I told myself. That's three months. It can't have been *three* months.

I concentrated on December first. My period usually came towards the end of the month. But at the end of December I'd gone to Les's that night when no one was home, and I hadn't had my period then.

I tried January next. I must've had it at the beginning of the month, instead of at the end of December, that's why I'd forgotten.

But I hadn't forgotten. At the beginning of January, Shanee and I took her sister Mabel to the water slides as a birthday treat. We'd gone in the water. I didn't use tampons; I couldn't have gone in the water if I'd had my period; everyone would've thought they were in *Jaws*.

I sat very still. I couldn't be pregnant. You can't get pregnant the first time, everybody knows that. I had living proof that it takes more than sticking a penis in you to make a baby straight away. My sister Dara had to be on her nine millionth time and she still wasn't pregnant. But if I was pregnant it had to have happened the first time, because we'd only ever really done it once. Plus, I hadn't had an orgasm, and I was pretty sure that you couldn't get pregnant without one. Besides, I wasn't throwing up every morning, was I? No, I wasn't. I felt absolutely fine. I didn't want to eat gherkins and chocolate ice cream either. I only cried when I argued with my mother. And my breasts weren't bigger. I didn't *feel* pregnant: I felt like *me*.

I tried to remember something – anything – from our sex education classes that would give me some clue about being pregnant. But I could only remember one thing: always use a condom.

Pink or Blue,
I Love You

"I don't see why I have to be the one to buy it," grumbled Shanee. She had her stubborn face on. It made her look about six.

"Because nobody would think for a second that you might be preggers, that's why," I said again. "They'll think it's for your mother."

Shanee grunted. "It might've been helpful if you'd thought for a second that you might get pregnant."

"Well, I didn't," I snapped. "I made a mistake."

Shanee was still looking stubborn.

"And what if Mr Arway in the chemist's says something to my mother?" she demanded. "What then?"

"Oh, for God's sake." Shanee was really beginning to get on my nerves. "What's he going to say?" I asked. "'Hello, Mrs Tyler. Was the pregnancy test positive?'" I gave her a shove. "Just *go*, will you? It'll be fine."

I pushed, but Shanee didn't budge.

"I'm embarrassed," she announced. "What if Mr Arway *doesn't* think it's for my mother? What if he thinks it's for *me*?" Everybody thought Shanee was so sweet, but she could have a really mean glare when she wanted to. "You can bet your trainers he'd say something to her then."

This was a little harder to argue with, since it was actually one of the reasons *I* wasn't willing to buy the pregnancy test myself. I didn't want the old cow to find out before I was ready to tell her.

"No, he wouldn't," I said reasonably. "Chemists are like doctors and priests. They aren't allowed to just blab out your personal secrets to anybody who comes down the street."

"Lucy Tyler isn't just anybody," said Shanee stubbornly. "She's my mother."

"I'll tell you what," I said, thinking quickly. "If it makes you feel any better, we'll catch the bus down to Oxford Street and you can buy it there."

The glare was replaced by a look of suspicion.

"*You* could buy it there, too," said my best friend since forever.

"No, *I* couldn't. Don't you get it? If *I* buy it, they'll be able to tell I'm the one who thinks she's pregnant, because I *am*. But they won't with you. You're innocent. It doesn't matter if anyone thinks you could be pregnant because you can't be."

"Innocent isn't the same as stupid."

I could feel my lower lip start to wobble.

"Please..." I begged. "Who else can I turn to?

You're the only real friend I've got." If I asked Gerri or Amie to do it, the whole planet would know the results before I did. "I can't face the chemist. Not in the state I'm in."

Which was a state of confusion. Now that I was over the shock, part of me (the part that would have to tell Hilary Spiggs) was definitely scared, but another part of me was feeling really excited. Like I was a child and it was Christmas Eve.

Shanee sighed. "I can't believe you didn't use a condom," she muttered. "I really can't. The government spends millions of pounds telling people to use condoms so they won't have babies they don't want, and you just jump right into bed without a second thought."

"You can't think when you're gripped by passion. It just takes over. You'll see for yourself, some day."

"No, I won't," said Shanee. "I'll've learnt my lesson from you."

I didn't open the bag once on the way home. Not even for a peek. I sat with it on my lap, while Shanee banged on about how the chemist had looked at her and how the other customers had looked at her and how the guard had smiled at her as she left.

I didn't open the bag until me and Shanee were safely locked in my bathroom.

"Oh, no," I cried. "It's the wrong kind. It's pink!"

"No, it isn't," said Shanee. "The applicator's

78

white. The indicator turns pink if you're knocked up."

"But the one Dara used was *blue*." I remembered it distinctly. I'd felt really chuffed at the time that Dara showed it to me and did the test while I was there, as if I wasn't her little sister but her friend.

Shance snatched the box out of my hand and tore it open.

"For God's sake, Lana. What difference does it make if it turns pink or blue? It means the same thing."

I took the applicator from her. "I know. I just want to make sure we got a good one, that's all."

"It was the most expensive one they had," said Shanee.

She unfolded the instructions and read them out to me. She turned her back while I peed. She stood beside me at the sink, staring at the applicator, waiting for something to happen or not happen.

Something happened. It turned pink.

"Maybe it's *wrong*," said Shanee at last.

I held up the carton. "It says it's as accurate as a doctor's test."

Shanee squashed her mouth together. "Well, of course it says *that*. It's not going to say, 'Not very accurate at all', is it?" She grabbed the applicator and held it up to the light. It was still pink.

"Maybe it's a dud," said Shanee.

I hadn't thought of that. The Spiggs was always buying things that didn't work. Hoovers, light bulbs, small appliances. It could happen with pregnancy tests, too.

"Do you think so? You think we should've got two?" I didn't want to make a mistake. This was really important.

Shanee sighed. "We'll get another one from a different shop." I could see the expression on her face in the mirror. She looked worried. And scared. "So we're sure."

Beside her, my face was already beginning to glow. I was that excited. Imagine, me pregnant! I couldn't believe it. I was going to be a mother. Talk about when I grow up! The only way I'd've felt more grown up was if I'd been the queen or somebody like that.

"Good idea," I agreed. "We'd better get two more." I dropped the applicator and the box into the Boots' bag. "If the next one is negative we'll have to do a third as a control."

Shanee's eyebrows rose.

"Good God!" said Shanee. "You have been paying some attention in science."

"I'll tell you one thing…" Shanee tossed the magazine she'd been pretending to flip through back on the coffee table. "I'm glad I don't have to tell your mother."

I heard her, but I didn't feel like speaking. I just couldn't get over it. When we did cooking, my rice pudding came out like soup. When we made clocks in design and technology, mine was too small to fit the timepiece. All my plants for the science project died. Twice. And yet I got pregnant, first time. It's like getting a hole in one the first time you pick up a golf club. But we'd done it. Me and Les. We were naturals. We were always meant to be.

Shanee twisted round so she was facing me.

"What are you going to do? I'm pretty sure you can get an abortion without your mum ever knowing."

"An abortion?" I had to laugh. "Are you joking? I'm not having an abortion."

Shanee blinked. "You're *not*?"

"Of course I'm not." I laughed again. "How could you think I would do something like that? This is my baby, Shanee! Mine and Les's. I'm not going to throw it out like an empty milk carton."

She just looked at me for a couple of minutes, as though I was Shakespeare or someone and she was trying to work out what I was *really* saying.

"You mean you're going to put it up for *adoption*?"

Putting your baby up for adoption was what the government thought teenage mothers should do. It was also the government who told us it was all right to eat beef and then all these people started acting like mad cows. I wasn't going to listen to the government.

I threw one of the couch cushions at her. "Now you're winding me up."

She held on to the cushion.

"You can't mean you're going to *keep* it," said

Shanee. She was speaking really slowly.

"Of course I'm going to keep it."

I hadn't *planned* to get pregnant because I hadn't thought that I *could*. But that didn't mean that it wasn't the right thing to do. Really, it was the solution to all my problems. Happiness was mine.

"This is what I've always wanted," I reminded her. I laughed. "Plus, having a baby beats taking my GCSEs."

"You can't take care of a baby, Lana!" Shanee was sitting so straight she looked like she might snap. "You're just a kid!"

I thought about the scrapbooks in the box under my bed. There was one that was filled with nothing but pictures of babies and little children. My ideal family was two boys and two girls; one of the boys and one of the girls was dark and the other two were fair. Which one would this be?

"I am not a kid." I got to my feet. "I'm a woman, Shanee. You may still be a kid, but I'm grown up." I stood up tall and proud. "I'm going to be a mother."

"You're going to be put in care, that's what you're going to be."

"Lots of girls our age have babies," I informed her coldly. "It's in all the papers. Plus, it's a definite advantage to be young with your children. Hilary was forty when she had me, and look how that turned out."

Shanee leaned forward. "Lana, for God's sake. This isn't like piercing your nose. This is really serious. Being a mother isn't a joke."

I sneered. "How would you know?"

"It just so happens that I would know." She stood up, too. "I've got two little brothers and a little sister, haven't I? I know exactly what it's like."

"They're not yours," I said. "It's different."

Nothing was stronger than the mother-child bond. Unless, of course, your mother happened to be like mine. But I wasn't like Hilary. I would be a great mother. I could already feel the connection between my baby and me starting to grow.

I patted my tummy. "I already love my baby, Shanee. Everything's going to be fine."

Her mouth was opened as though she was putting on lipgloss. "I want you to know that I think you're mad. Totally bonkers."

"You're the one who's bonkers. This is the best thing that ever happened to me."

Shanee was shaking her head and waving her hands about. "I have to go home. I'm too traumatized to have this discussion now."

She was traumatized? How did she think I felt?

"What about me?" I snapped. "I'm the one who has to tell Les. You know what men are like. They think babies are a trap."

Shanee picked up her things and gave me a "poor little cow" sort of look.

"Men aren't the only ones," said Shanee. "So does my mother." She put her bag over her shoulder. "And so do I."

I liked the idea of no one else knowing about the baby for a while. I felt like I had this brilliant secret – like I knew where the Ark of the Covenant really was or something like that – and it made me feel really happy and in charge.

So I bunked off school for the next couple of days. I didn't feel like going even more than usual. I mean, what was the point? I wasn't going to finish, was I? I didn't even have to pretend any more. We'd see who was the poor cow. A year from now, when Shanee was studying herself into a coma, I was going to be pushing my baby up the high street in a blue and yellow pushchair with a basket at the back for the shopping and wondering what to make Les for supper.

Plus, now that I knew I was pregnant for certain, I reckoned I should take care of myself. Taking care of yourself during pregnancy is very important. Running around a hockey pitch and being yelled at by teachers *was not* taking care of myself. Besides, now that I knew I had a baby inside me, I *felt* really pregnant. I was tired and didn't want to do very much. I had to pee a lot. I had sudden cravings for everything from chocolate to that special sauce they put on the burgers in Burger King. Sad songs made me feel like crying. I came over all weak whenever I saw an infant.

So, every morning I'd get up, get dressed, have my breakfast, and put on my coat. I'd pick up my school bag, make sure I had my keys, and give my mother a big wave goodbye. Then I'd go to McDonald's or Burger King, till I was sure Hilary had left for work. And then I went back home.

I spent my days watching telly and thinking about babies. There was a lot to think about. Should I breast-feed? It was easier than bottles, since you didn't have to wash anything, but it also meant that I couldn't go anywhere without the baby for more than a couple of hours. What if Les wanted to take me away for a weekend or something? Then there was the problem of where it should sleep. Should it sleep with me and Les at the beginning, or should it have a room of its own? What colour would I paint its room? Pink and blue were out, they were tacky. Yellow was OK, but it had to be a restful shade. I wondered if Les knew how to put up shelves. We'd need shelves for its toys and stuff.

And I'd need something to carry it around in. I'd seen women carrying babies in backpacks but that was a bit primitive, if you asked me. What I really wanted was one of those big old-fashioned prams with lots of chrome, but I could see that that wouldn't be practical. I mean, it'd be hard to get it on a bus. But I could get an ordinary pushchair for everyday and save the pram for Sunday walks in the park. And then there were clothes. Clothes were important. Should I shop at Mothercare or Baby Gap?

Shanee came round on her way home from school every afternoon with my homework. As if I was really going to do it. But no matter what I said, she refused to get real about my situation.

"You can't stay indoors for ever," she kept saying. "You have to tell them some time."

"I will," I said. "I'm going to. I just don't see what the big rush is."

She goggled her eyes. "You don't? Hasn't it occurred to you that the longer you wait, the less options you have?"

"But I don't need any options. I told you. I want this baby. It's all settled." I patted my tummy. "I'm happy, Shanee. This really is the best thing that ever happened to me."

"If you're so happy, then tell its grandmother and father," begged Shanee. "You're driving me mad."

"I will," I promised. "I'll tell the old bat first."

I had no doubt about how Hilary would react. Charley said she was very volatile, which meant she started screaming before you'd finished talking, and thought about it later. When I told *her* she was going to be a grandmother she'd go into meltdown. But that was all she'd do. She'd march around in one of her moods, slamming doors and banging things on tables for a while. She'd start screaming at every chance she got. She'd talk to my nan and my sisters on the phone for hours, and then blame me because the bill was so high. But in the end she'd shut up. I mean, what could she do? She was a cow, but she wasn't going to throw me out on the street. Charley wouldn't let her.

But I wasn't *totally* sure about Les. That's why I reckoned I'd save him for last. I mean, I knew he was the hard-working, responsible type. He had a job and a flat and everything, and he'd never missed one of his car loan repayments. Not one. Plus, he was well chuffed not to be a virgin any more. A man like that might be thrilled to hear that he'd scored a goal. That sort of thing is important to guys. But it *was* a little unexpected. A year ago he was still sleeping in the room he'd had since he was born and now he was going to be a dad. He might freak out a bit when he found out. Because of the suddenness and all. Especially since Les's dream was to own a Porsche someday. A cherry red convertible. A cherry red convertible Porsche isn't exactly a family car.

"When?" persisted Shanee.

"As soon as I have a chance."

My Chances Come

The phone rang that night, while Dragon Lady and I were eating in front of the telly.

I didn't move. I knew it wasn't for me. Neither Les nor Shanee would ring that early. Les because he was at work, and Shanee because the Tyler circus would be in full swing at that hour.

Huffing and puffing, she heaved herself from her chair and went to answer it. When she came back she marched straight up to the screen and snapped it off.

"Hey!" I shouted. "I was watching that!"

"And I should've been watching *you*," said my mother. She folded her arms in front of her so she looked like a wall in jeans and a pink sweatshirt. A pissed-off wall. "Just where the hell have you been for the last three days when you should've been at school?"

I stared back. "What are you talking about?"

"Don't give me that," said my mother. "You

88

know exactly what I'm talking about. You haven't been to school for three days."

I swear to God, she started tapping her foot. And she thought *I* watched too many films!

"'Course I have."

Sometimes bluffing worked. I was really good at looking blank and sincere. It confused her. Even though she hated everything about me, part of her didn't want to think her daughter was a liar.

But it didn't work this time.

"Oh no, you haven't." She jerked her head towards the kitchen. "That was Mrs Mela. She says you haven't been in since Tuesday."

"I told you. I don't like Shakespeare."

It was incredible how thin she could make her lips when she wanted to.

"To *school*. Not just to English."

"You mean *this* week?"

Taptaptaptaptap. Fred Astaire would've loved her.

"Yes, I mean this week. Why weren't you at school?"

I shrugged. "I didn't feel like going."

"You didn't feel like going..." Hilary the Parrot.

"That's right." I got up and moved towards her, to put the telly back on. "I was feeling too stressed."

She cackled. "Too *stressed*? *You*?" She flattened herself against the screen. "You think stress is breaking a nail or getting some mud on your jeans."

"What do you know?"

I made a move towards the TV, but she pushed me back and I whacked into the coffee table. I screamed in pain.

She didn't care that she'd wounded me. "I know you've been bunking off school, that's what I know. And I'd like to know why."

I rubbed the back of my leg.

"I hope you're happy," I snapped. "You've really hurt me."

"Not yet, I haven't," she screeched. "But I will if you don't start giving me some straight answers."

I stood up tall. My tummy stuck out in the air between us.

"I told you. I didn't feel like going. That's all."

"No, it isn't *all*," said PC Hilary Spiggs. "I want to know where you were."

I was the same height as her. I stared right into those beady eyes.

"I was here, that's where I was. Satisfied?"

She wasn't satisfied. She started banging on about her responsibility as a parent, and my responsibility as a young adult, and what a mess my future was going to be if I got expelled for absenteeism.

"My responsibilities as a *young adult*?" I screamed back. "That's a laugh. I'm not a young adult to you. To you I'm still a little kid."

"You get treated the way you act," said my mother.

And that's when I told her. Just like that. It

seemed like the right moment.

"Oh, yeah?" I gave her my smuggest smile. "Well, for your information it just so happens that *I'm* having a baby." I stepped up my smile. "How's that for acting grown up?"

She just stood there staring back at me, looking like I'd bashed her over the head with a dead fish. Then she smiled the way people do in films when they've been bashed over the head with a dead fish – or knifed.

"You're not serious." There was a squeaky laugh in her voice. "You're winding me up. Aren't you, Lana? You're not really pregnant."

"Oh, yes I am." I held up my fingers. "Three months."

"But you couldn't—"

"S–E–X," I spelt it out for her. "That's how you do it, in case you forgot."

I could tell she didn't think I was lying now.

She took a really deep breath and chewed on her lip for a couple of seconds.

Then, as if we were discussing a school trip or something, she said, "I'll make some tea. We have to sit down and decide what's best to do. Have you been to the doctor?"

I shook my head.

She was already halfway to the kitchen.

"We'd better get you over there first thing. Make sure everything's all right." The kitchen's just off the living-room, so I could see her grab the kettle and bang it against the sink. "It's not too late to have it taken care of."

You'd think she was talking about having the dog put down.

"I'm not having an abortion if that's what you mean," I shouted over the running of the tap.

She turned off the water and looked over her shoulder. "You what?"

"I'm not killing my baby," I said loudly. "I'm having it."

She cradled the kettle in her arms. She could do a pretty good blank face when she wanted to, too.

"I don't suppose this means you're going to put it up for adoption."

She was dead calm, like a telly that's been switched off.

"Of course not. It's my baby. I'm keeping it."

She suddenly realized she was still holding the kettle. She put it on the counter as though it was made of glass.

"And what about the father?"

"What about him?"

"Is this his decision, too?"

"It's *my* decision. I'm the one who's pregnant."

"But what about the father?" she said again. She was nothing if not stubborn "Where is he?" Her mouth was a straight line. "Better yet, *who* is he?"

That's all I needed. When I was in primary school, the neighbour's dog got our dog pregnant. As soon as the puppies were weaned, Hilary

Spiggs put them all in a box and left them on the Scudders' doorstep. She said she'd done her bit, now they could do theirs. I didn't want her leaving my baby on Les's doorstep with a note pinned to its blanket, *Your turn now.*

"It's none of your business who he is," I said. "You'll only ruin everything."

She could still laugh. "*I'll* ruin everything. And what is it you think you're doing?"

I held my head high. "I'm a grown-up now. I can take care of myself."

"You don't seem to be doing a very good job," said my mother. "If you could take care of yourself you would have taken some precautions."

"Maybe I didn't want to take precautions."

She wasn't expecting that. "Are you saying you did this deliberately? You deliberately got yourself pregnant?"

My expression was emotionless. Let her think what she wanted.

"I don't believe this." Her voice cracked. "You're fifteen years old. You've got your whole life ahead of you. You don't want to saddle yourself with a child—"

"You mean like you were saddled with me?" I shouted. I was probably lucky she hadn't left *me* on someone's doorstep. I started crying. "Is that what you mean?"

She went dead still for a second and then her whole face sort of caved in. "Oh, Lana, plea— I know I've made a lot of mistakes. It wasn't easy

93

after your dad left … at my age … living with Nan … trying to work out what to do next… We'd lost everything—"

"I suppose that was *my* fault too!" I shrieked. When Charlene and Dara's dad died, he left insurance money and a house and things like that behind. When my dad went off, he left the debts of a small Third World country and a queue of bailiffs and policemen behind. Plus, Charlene and Dara were clever and motivated like their dad, and I wasn't. "You've always blamed me for my dad. You look at me and all you see is a big mistake!"

"That's not true, Lana." She made a move to touch me, but I pulled away. "You're the proof—"

I didn't want to hear her lies.

"Well, I'm not like you," I screamed. "I already love my baby. And I'm not killing it. Or giving it away. And it's never going to have to be on its own."

She looked like she was trying not to cry. She started saying all the usual stuff about how much responsibility a child is and how hard it is to bring one up on your own, but I wasn't going to listen. I grabbed my jacket from the arm of the couch and shot out the door.

I went straight to Blockbuster.

There were a few customers strolling past the new releases, and a boy and a girl behind the desk with Les.

He gave me a wave.

"You read my mind," he called. "I was thinking

of taking a break. Do you fancy a coffee?"

We sat at *our* table in McDonald's, in the corner by the window.

Les had had a big fight with a customer who said he'd brought back a video that he hadn't brought back.

"People!" He shook his head. "You'd be amazed at what they try on."

"I know." I'd stopped crying by then, but I snuffled a bit so he'd know I was upset. "It's incredible."

He looked at me over his coffee. "You OK? Your eyes look funny."

I glanced in the mirror behind him. I looked like a panda.

"I had another fight with Witch Hilary." I wiped at my eyes with the back of my hand. "My mascara's run."

"What about this time?" Les grinned. "Did you forget to buy the milk again?"

"Not exactly." I looked into my cup. "Can I go home with you tonight? I'll tell you what happened then."

Coffee sloshed over the sides of Les's cup.

"To *my* place? Tonight?"

I handed him my napkin. "It was a really big fight. I don't want to go home." I gave him a stern but affectionate smile. "I've really got to talk to you."

He was busy mopping up the table. "Not tonight, Lana. It's impossible tonight."

"But I can't go home." My voice was a little shriller than I'd meant it to be. "Please let me stay with you."

He was shaking his head. "Another time, but not tonight."

"But I've got to talk to you!"

He blinked. I'd never shouted at *him* before.

"Well, here I am," said Les. "Talk to me."

I like McDonald's, I really do. And I know McDonald's really likes kids and everything. But it still isn't the sort of place where you announce that you're pregnant.

"Not here," I said. "Somewhere private."

Les waved his arm. "This is private. There's no one near enough to hear us."

He gave me a look. Now we were even. I'd never seen him pissed off with me before either.

"If you keep your voice down," he added meaningfully.

I ignored him.

"*Why* is it impossible tonight?" I demanded. "It'll be late. No one'll even know that I'm there."

He paid no attention.

"So what was the fight about? How come you need to talk to me?"

I pushed my drink away. "I want to go home with you."

"And I've told you, you can't." He glanced at his watch. "I've got to get back. We've got a trainee tonight."

"What about our talk?"

He got up and pushed in his chair. "Talk on the way to the shop, or it'll have to wait."

"It can't wait. My biological clock is ticking."

Les laughed. "What are you on about now?"

I sat up straight. I folded my hands on the table in front of me.

"Les," I said. "I'm going to have a baby."

He laughed again. "Yeah, course you are."

"I am," I said. "Your baby. Ours."

He sat back down.

"Jesus," said Les. "I can't believe this. I thought you were on the pill."

Why would he think that?

"But you knew I was a virgin. Why would I be on the pill?"

He stared back at me as if I was a difficult customer.

"I thought you had it sorted. That night when I came after the stag party … I thought…" He shrugged. "I thought you were, you know, ready…"

"I was ready…"

I started to cry again. It wasn't like you could just go to the chemist and buy a packet of birth control pills like a pregnancy test, was it?

"But I wasn't on the pill."

Les reached out and put his hands on mine. "Do you want me to go to the clinic with you? I'll go if you want. You shouldn't go alone."

I swallowed some tears. "What clinic?"

97

"For the abortion," said Les. He squeezed my fingers. "I won't let you go on your own."

This was not in my script.

"But I'm not having an abortion." I smiled through the teardrops. "I'm keeping the baby."

"Keeping the baby?" You'd think my hands had turned into hot coals, he took his away so fast. "Are you nuts? You want to have a baby? What about your A levels? What about going to RADA and all that? You can't have a baby now."

That was what I'd told Les, that I was doing my A levels and applying to RADA when I finished. I was surprised he'd remembered. Since I hadn't.

"Yes, I can," I said. "I always planned to have children. I'm just starting a little sooner than I thought."

"And what about *me*?" hissed Les. "I told you right from the start, Lana, I'm not ready for anything serious." He was wearing a deep orange shirt and a black and orange tie. He fiddled with the tie. "I'm only twenty, for Christ's sake. I'm not ready for a kid. I'm just getting my career off the ground. I can't support you and *it*. I can barely support myself."

"I'm not asking you to support us," I said stiffly. "I'm not trying to trap you, Les. And I won't tell Hilary who the dad is, if that's what you're worried about. You can count on that." I looked deep into his eyes. "But let's not forget who didn't bother using a condom."

He blushed and looked at his hands. "Don't I

have any say in this?"

I swallowed hard. "You can say what you want, but I'm not killing our baby." I raised my chin. "And I'm not giving it away either."

Les squashed his coffee cup in his palms. "And just how do I know that it's *our* baby, Lana? Huh? How do I know *that*?"

This wasn't in my script, either.

"What do you mean?" I wasn't keeping my voice down. I was trying to, but it wasn't possible. "Of course it's yours! I was a *virgin*! Do you think the father's *God*?"

"For Christ's sake, Lana!" hissed Les. "Everybody can hear you."

"I didn't want to discuss this here," I shrieked. "I wanted to go to your place. So we could have a proper talk."

"Well, you can't come round tonight." His eyes shifted. "It's Gary. Gary's having a party. It'd be worse than trying to talk in here."

"But we can go to your room—"

He looked at his watch again. "I've got to get back, Lana. I'm sorry. Are you coming?"

I'd never seen Les look so cold and hard. He was like a stranger. I hadn't thought about it before, but all of a sudden it hit me that I could lose him. If I caused him too much trouble... Instead of us getting married and having our own flat, he could get a transfer south of the river or something and I'd never see him again. I took a tissue from my pocket and blew my nose.

"I can't believe it," I mumbled. "You're angry with me!"

"I'm not angry, Lana. I just... It's a bit of a shock, that's all." He came round and put a hand on my shoulder. "You're sure your mother doesn't know about me?"

I nodded. "Of course she doesn't. It's none of her business who the dad is, is it?"

"And you're sure it's mine?"

My tears fell on his hand.

I couldn't tell if I had more chance of losing him if he knew he *was* the father, or more chance if he thought it could be someone else. I decided to hedge my bets.

"As sure as a woman can be," I said truthfully.

Let him work out what that meant for himself.

And that was it, really.

Except for the part where I got tortured as punishment for becoming a grown-up without anyone's permission. The form of torture chosen by my mother was having to listen to advice from everyone and anyone she could drag into my private affairs.

Nan said I didn't know what I was letting myself in for.

"Children are a full-time job," said my nan. "Just washing the nappies used to take me hours."

I thought she was joking. It had never occurred to me that disposable nappies hadn't always been around.

"Well, nobody washes nappies any more," I said when she'd corrected me. "*Or* bottles."

"You're throwing your life away," said my nan.

"You mean like *you* did?" I asked. "You had four kids. That means you threw it away more than once."

"You should learn from other people's mistakes," said my nan. "Not repeat them."

My sister Charlene had obviously inherited her genes from my mother's side.

"You're throwing your life away," said Charlene. "You should live a little before you have kids."

"You've got two of your own," I pointed out.

"You don't have a husband," said Charlene.

"Neither do you. You're divorced."

"Thanks for reminding me," said Charlene. "But I *do* have someone who contributes to our expenses. *And* I have a job. I'd go mad if I had to stay at home with them."

I laughed. "You're mad, anyway."

My sister Dara – the one who'd been trying to have a baby for about twenty years – said my life was over.

"You're the one who said there's more to life than a good job and a gold credit card," I reminded her. It was the song she sang at every family gathering after her second glass of wine. "You're the one who wants to get knocked up so bad."

"I'm not fifteen," said Dara. "I've travelled and

stuff. I have a career and a stable relationship. All you do is go shopping and watch telly."

The headteacher said I didn't *have* to give up school and my GCSEs. The door to my education wasn't closed. There were special programmes for girls in my situation.

"What situation?" I asked. "I haven't been kid-napped. I'm having a baby."

The doctor said she hoped I knew what I was doing and that there were people I could talk to if I couldn't talk to my mother.

"Make sure you explore all your options," she advised me.

"I have," I said. "I'm not a murderer."

They all sounded like my mother when they sighed.

The doctor gave me a stack of leaflets to read, vitamins and a regular appointment at the antena-tal clinic. She told me there were birthing classes at the hospital me and my partner could sign up for.

I said my partner and I would be keen.

"It'll take a lot of the mystery and fear out of it for you," she informed me. "I'd strongly recom-mend it. Especially since you're so young."

"We'll go," I promised. "We consider this a sharing experience."

I got that line from a magazine for mothers-to-be. Old four-eyes loved it.

Then she told me all about the toy library and the clothing exchange the council ran. As if I'd let my child play with toys some other kids had chewed on or wear clothes somebody else's baby had had the splatters in. I mean, really…

Even Mrs Mugurdy upstairs got in on the act. She thought I was throwing my life away, too.

"When I was your age I was dreaming of sailing across the ocean to Thailand or Peru," said Mrs Mugurdy, "not watching *Sesame Street*."

"And here you are in Kilburn," I answered cheerfully.

"I did live in Singapore for many years," said Mrs Mugurdy.

I thought she was winding me up. I didn't know Singapore was a country, I thought it was some kind of drink.

Only Charley didn't give me a hard time.

"I rather fancy being a grandad," said Charley. "I like babies."

"That's because you've never had any," said my mother.

Preggers

I had my own ideas of what being preggers would be like.

My body would swell, but it would be more womanly and sensual. With all those hormones steaming through my body, my skin would become soft and radiant. I would *glow*.

It wouldn't all be good news, though. There was morning sickness and indigestion and various aches and pains. The old cow made sure I knew all about those.

"Just wait till you get heartburn," she'd tell me gleefully. "Just wait till you can't sleep or sit down for more than five minutes."

But what I was worried about was becoming frumpy and tired-looking like some of the women I saw in the supermarket. I'd look at them and think, how could *they* get pregnant when they're so unattractive?

And I wasn't going to walk as though someone

had stuck my arms on backwards, either. I'd seen a picture of Cindy Crawford naked when she was pregnant, and she looked great. And pictures of Posh Spice. She had clothes on, but they were cool designer clothes, and she looked great, too. You couldn't imagine them crouching over the toilet bowl or refusing to go to a party because their back hurt. They were beautiful *and* pregnant. Not pregnant but beautiful. That's what I was going to be like.

I could see myself sort of floating down Oxford Street in a long, flowing white dress. I was wearing gold platforms and a gold necklace and the gold charm bracelet Les gave me for Christmas. Women smiled at me. Men gazed longingly. When I got on a bus *everybody* offered me a seat. Light shimmered around me and everyone was laughing. I looked like an angel with a bun in the oven and a lot of friends.

"Lana!" my mother shouted through the bathroom door. "Lana, are you all right?"

If my mouth hadn't been filled with vomit I'd've made some snappy answer to shut her up. Like, "I'm fine. This is what I do instead of having a second cup of tea." It wasn't even morning sickness, really. I got it all the time, morning, noon and night.

But my mouth *was* filled with vomit so I just gagged.

"Do you want me to make you a cup of tea before I go?"

I swear, the woman was a tea junkie. You wouldn't want to be on the *Titanic* with *her*. Instead of a life-jacket, she'd throw you a cup of PG Tips.

"Agggh!" I choked in reply.

"Are you sure?"

"Yeah," I gasped. "I'm brilliant."

I spat the remains of my breakfast into the bowl, rinsed my mouth with the glass of water I kept next to the loo for these emergencies and shuffled to the door.

She was still there.

"Are you going to school?"

She thought I should stay till the end of the year. To make sure that I did, she was blackmailing me. If I didn't make an effort to go to school, even if I was puking up all over the place, she'd cut off my pocket-money.

"Do I have a choice?"

She wasn't exactly subtle.

"No," she said. "You don't."

I glared. "Well then…"

"*This* is what it means to be grown up," she informed me. "You made your bed, and now you're going to have to lie in it."

I didn't say anything. I hoped she could see in my eyes how much I hated her.

"Though knowing you, I shouldn't think you actually made the bed first," said my mother.

* * *

106

After the Spiggs left I got dressed.

I used to look forward to getting dressed in the morning. What mood was I in? What colours should I wear? You know, that sort of thing.

But not any more.

The only mood I was ever in was pregnant. My tummy was as big as a basketball, my breasts were like melons and my bum looked like it was padded. The only good thing about any of this was the breasts. Les was a breast man. He thought my breasts were great this size.

I stood in front of the full-length mirror on the back of my door.

I didn't look like Cindy Crawford *or* Posh Spice. I looked like an inflatable girl that had gone wrong.

Plus, I didn't have much that really fitted me any more. Stretch jeans and miniskirts aren't exactly designed for a bulging body. And maternity clothes are. Which means that you might as well wear a dustbin bag with holes cut out for your arms. I'd seen a few pregnant women in dresses that actually showed the bulge, but there was no way I could go to school like that, it was asking for trouble.

I'd blown most of my savings on a maternity dress that was really cool. I found it in this trendy boutique for mothers-to-be. It was a knee-length A-line with a square neck and long sleeves, and an adjustable belt thing that tied high up at the back so you could wear it even after you had the baby. It came in green or blue. I reckoned green might make me look too much like a moving hillock, so I got it in blue. As per usual, Hilary Spiggs went mad when she found out how much I'd paid for it. *She* wanted me to wear the old junk she brought home. But I looked great in the dress. Only I couldn't wear it every day, could I? I *never* wore the same thing twice in a row, unless it was pyjamas. I wasn't going to let pregnancy force me to drop my standards.

The doorbell rang while I was trying on a heavy black jumper Charley'd left behind. It was so big that I didn't look pregnant, I looked like I was swimming in treacle. I could leave my flies open and no one would ever know.

"I didn't realize the 'builder' look was in this season," said Shanee when I answered the door.

She used to wait for me at the post-box on the corner, but now she called at the house. I wasn't sure if the Wicked Witch had put her up to it – to make sure I went to school – or if it really was because she got tired of waiting so long for me to get ready.

I struck a model-like pose.

"Am I radiant?" I gushed.

Pregnant women were supposed to shine like a radium dial. Everybody said so.

Shanee tilted her head on one side. "Well," she said, "you do have a few more zits."

It was all right for the headteacher and Hilary Spiggs to say I should stay at school. They didn't have to put up with the teasing and taunting.

"What's that you've got under your jumper, Lana?" shouted one of the Year Eights as Shanee and I walked into the building. "You smuggling footballs into school?"

So funny I forgot to laugh.

Sometimes it was footballs. Sometimes it was melons. Other times, they'd just laugh, without saying anything.

I wasn't going to look over to count them, but there were about three of the pimply little cretins hanging out by the entrance. They were practically wetting themselves, they thought they were so hysterical.

"Ignore them," said Shanee. "They're baby dorks."

It was what Shanee always said.

The baby dorks weren't the worst, though. The worst were the older dorks. There were a couple of the real hard cases who would kind of slide up to me if I was on my own, smiling and drooling. "I hear pregnant women are always horny...," they'd say. Or, "I hear pregnant women are really desperate..." Or, "How about letting me have a taste of your milk?" Rude stuff like that.

"They'll get tired of it eventually," said Shanee.

This was also what she always said.

I didn't say anything. A hot bubble of something that wasn't quite air and wasn't quite water had lodged itself in my throat. "Loo," I muttered. "I think I'm going to be sick."

We headed for the loo.

There were about a million girls stuffed into the toilet. It sounded like a hut full of chickens. A couple of girls were actually using the cubicles, but most of them were squashed together at the sinks, checking their make-up in the mirrors.

"Jesus," Shanee groaned. "You couldn't get a lizard through here." She glanced at me anxiously. "Can you wait?"

I clapped my hand over my mouth and shook my head.

"Coming through!" shouted Shanee. "Coming through!"

No one so much as looked over. They were all too busy with getting their eyes right and admiring each other's clothes. Normally, I'd've been with them.

I forced my way in. There was a free toilet right at the end, but I couldn't get to it.

The hot bubble was beginning to burst.

I choked.

"She's going to be sick!" screamed Shanee. "Get out of the way. She's going to be sick!"

The girl who was blocking my way made a face, but she flattened herself against the girl in front of her, holding her mascara wand in the air like a flag.

"Jesus," she muttered. "No wonder everybody warns you about having sex."

* * *

"So, Saturday," Gerri was saying. "We'll blitz the lot. Miss Selfridge, Hennes, Gap..." She winked at Shanee. "We can even hit the Notting Hill Housing Trust Charity Shop if you want."

Amie opened her packet of crisps. Cheese and onion. The smell was enough to make me gag.

"Sounds great to me. I want to get a top like that one we saw in *Cosmo*. You know, with the V-neck and the stripes?"

I chewed on a plain water biscuit and tried not to yawn.

I was used to school being boring, but not *lunch*, for God's sake.

"It's tempting," said Shanee. "I got a brilliant denim jacket in the Trust last time we went. But I can't go on Saturday." She made the face of someone who has suffered a lot. "I've got to mind the brats."

"Bring 'em with you," said Gerri. "We can handle three of them between us."

Shanee groaned. "You've got to be kidding! I'd rather take a bear shopping with me. It'd behave better and we'd get on the news."

Gerri turned to me. "What about you, Lana? You can still squeeze through the aisles, can't you?"

"Oh, hahaha." I bit into another biscuit. "Actually, maybe I will come along. I want to check out Mothercare. It's time I started thinking about his clothes."

"What makes you think it's going to be a boy?" asked Gerri.

"I just know." I shrugged. "You have a feeling about these things."

Amie choked. "I'd've thought you'd've had enough of feelings."

"And I should probably check out the baby books…" I went on. "I still haven't decided about breast-feeding."

"Please, no … no more about breast-feeding."

To my surprise, it was Shanee who was holding up her hand and looking pained.

"Am I being a breast-feeding bore?" I enquired. "Is that what you're trying to say?"

Amie and Gerri both looked at Shanee.

"Well, you do bang on about it," she said defensively.

"Among other things," mumbled Gerri.

Amie started humming "Rock-a-bye Baby" under her breath.

"But it's important." Now I was the one who sounded defensive. "It can mess up a kid for life if you get it wrong."

"That doesn't mean you have to talk about it all the time," said Shanee. "Talk about something else."

I couldn't talk about something else. Most of my topics of conversation had dried up. I didn't even see that many films any more. The cinema seats were too uncomfortable for more than a few minutes. And, in case you're interested in irony, now that I had a free source of videos I always fell asleep on the couch before they were over.

"Like wha—" I began. But I didn't get any further. Another bubble was rising in my throat. My mouth felt like a cup of half-finished hot chocolate that had been left under the bed for a couple of weeks.

"God!" I gasped, and jumped to my feet, scattering the rest of my lunch on the ground. "I'm going to be sick again."

Gerri groaned. "You'd think you'd carry a stack of sick bags with you," she said.

There was one person I never complained to, and that was Les. Not about all the regular general aches and pains, or the morning sickness, or the indigestion, or the sore tits, or anything like that. I didn't want him to think I was a whingeing pregnant woman. If I felt like I was going to puke, I didn't gag and choke and rush off with my hand clamped over my mouth the way I would've if I was with Hilary or Shanee. I excused myself with a smile and a vague grunt and just wafted away. I ran once I was out of his sight. And I always turned the tap on in the bath when I had to be sick, so he wouldn't hear. I never talked about nappies or breast-feeding or anything like that with Les, either. I mean, Shanee complained and she was a girl, it should've been interesting to her. I didn't want to bore Les or make him think I expected him to go shopping for stuff for the baby.

And there was one part of my life that pregnancy actually improved.

My sex life. I hadn't realized before that certain men found pregnant women a real turn-on, but they did. Les said pregnant women were sort of exotic and exciting. He said none of his friends had ever made it with a pregnant woman. They were all really curious about it. And jealous.

"Imagine," he said. "*Me*, the boy in my year voted most likely never to have sex. What a hoot."

Hilary and Charley finally got back together around Easter, and, as soon as they did, Les started dropping round after work again.

At first he'd have a beer, eat a takeaway and watch the news or the football before we got into a clinch, but after a while he didn't even bother to eat.

He thought my breasts and my bum were fantastic. "Now that's what I call a real handful," he'd say admiringly.

It was almost surprising that he actually understood I was pregnant. For all he ever said about it, he might have thought I was just putting on weight. We never talked about me being pregnant except in connection to the size of some of my external parts. It was a wonder, as my nan would say. A real wonder. I looked at myself and started counting the months before I could get into real clothes again, but Les looked at me and saw a sex goddess. A sex goddess who couldn't get knocked up.

"Natural birth control," is how Les put it. "Sex without fear." He grinned. "And without condoms." Les didn't like condoms, he said it wasn't the same. He obviously didn't know from personal experience, but that was what his friends told him.

I was happy to be his sex goddess. Even if most of the time I felt more like hell's plaything, it was great for my ego. For someone who'd been a little slow in getting started, Les was making up for lost time. He was always hugging and stroking me, and he'd have to be really tired or pissed not to want what he called "a quick roll in the hay".

That's why I thought that when Les started talking about his summer holiday he meant we were going away together. To somewhere romantic with room service where we could make love for hours instead of minutes just in case the Spiggs came home unexpectedly.

We even looked through the brochures together: Greece, Italy, Cyprus, Spain... To be honest, they all looked pretty much the same – a blue blob of water, a blob of sand dotted with bodies, and a hotel – but I didn't care *where* we went. I knew wherever we went, we'd find a private lagoon with a palm tree and water the same blue as my good maternity dress.

Then one night Les turned up with a bottle of fizzy wine.

"What's the occasion?" I asked as he unscrewed the top.

"You won't believe it, but I've been sort of promoted. They're transferring me to Finsbury Park."

He puffed out his chest. "Manager." He laughed. "That makes me the youngest manager in the company."

I forced a happy smile on to my face. This *was* good news. Les was a manager at only twenty-one. He'd be a director or something by thirty. We'd live in the suburbs and I'd have a four-wheel drive with tinted windows and lots of kids and dogs in the back. But I couldn't be that happy about it *now*. It meant I could never just drop by the shop any more. It meant he had further to come.

"But that's not all." Les grinned. "They finally agreed my holiday time. I booked my package this morning."

I didn't hear "my". I heard "our".

"Really?" I couldn't exactly bounce with excitement (not without knocking something over), but there was excitement in my voice. "Where are we going? When?"

Les stopped pouring.

"*We*?"

"I'm going with you, aren't I?" I thought he was joking. "Remember we looked at the brochures?"

He thought *I* was joking.

He laughed. "Get real, Lana. I can't take you to Greece. You know that."

Did I?

"Do I?"

He rolled his eyes the way Charley does when Hilary can't find her keys and has to take everything out of her handbag *again*.

"Of course you do. I've only got two weeks, you know." His eyes moved from my face to my tummy, looming in the space between us like a giant balloon. "You can't fly with a bun in the oven. Not when you're as far gone as you are. Everybody knows that." He laughed again. "And there's no way I'm taking a bus to Greece."

I laughed along, as though I really had been joking. I *didn't* know about not being able to fly at the end of your pregnancy, but now that he said it, it sort of made sense. But it would never have occurred to me that Les would book his holiday for when I couldn't go. If anything, I thought he'd have waited till *after* the baby was born and we could give him to my nan to look after while we went away. She had nothing else to do.

If Charley told Hilary he was going on holiday without her she'd have gone ballistic. She'd've made his life hell and never shut up till he gave in. But I wasn't like *her*. I was understanding and tolerant. I knew that a man needs outside interests and friends of his own. I was tolerant of his need for space. I sucked back some tears.

"Oh," I said. "Well, Greece sounds like it should be fun."

"It sure as hell should be," said Les. He took a large gulp of his wine. "I can't wait."

I took a tiny sip from my glass. I could tell by the smell that it was going to give me indigestion.

"So," I said brightly. "When are you going?"

"End of August. That way I get an extra day with the bank holiday."

But not enough extra to go by bus, obviously.

"End of August," I echoed. The end of August was when the baby was due. I touched my glass to his. "Well, I hope you have a good time."

Wrenching My Guts Out, Wish You Were Here

I had an appointment at the clinic four days before I reckoned the baby would be born. I put on my cool maternity outfit, but the only shoes that were really comfortable were my trainers, which kind of ruined the effect. I put on my make-up and tied my hair back, which made me look older. Then I put some dance music in my Discman and practically skipped to the practice, I was that happy. Only a few more days and I wouldn't be pregnant any more. I couldn't wait. I felt like I'd been pregnant most of my life by now. It was hard to remember being able to sit at the table for more than five minutes before my back started aching. It was even harder to remember being able to have a cup of tea without feeling like somebody was pouring acid in my blood. But soon that would all be over and things would go back to normal. The best part was about to begin.

The doctor told me off for not going to the birthing classes.

"I thought you promised me you'd try and go."

It was more a question than a statement.

"I know I did," I said. It was incredible how many people sounded just like my mother. "And we were going to, really, but my boyfriend had to go to the States for a few months. For work. It was sudden."

She peered at me over her glasses. "You could have gone on your own."

I smiled, sort of shy and embarrassed. "I didn't fancy going without him." Which I didn't.

"It's not too late," said the doctor. "There's a class next week."

By next week I shouldn't need any classes. By then I'd be a mother.

Or maybe not.

The doctor said I'd got the date wrong.

"The baby seems small, Lana. Do you think you could have made a mistake?"

I said I supposed I could have.

"This is all new to me," I joked.

She gave me a Queen Victoria smile. You know, like it hurt.

"Well, you're doing very well," she assured me. But the baby wouldn't come until September. "Virgo," she said. "That's a good sign."

I got a book on horoscopes out of the library on my way home, so I could see for myself whether Virgo was a good sign or not. I didn't have much else to do. It was the summer holidays, wasn't it? Shanee and her family had gone to her grandad's in Ireland for a few weeks. Les was in Greece with his mates. Even Gerri and Amie were away.

Plus, I already had everything ready for the baby. It was laid out in my room. My nan bought me a cot, and Charley bought me a pushchair, and my sisters bought me a load of clothes, all in yellow or green, since they didn't believe I was definitely having a boy. I'd decided against breast-feeding because I reckoned I was bound to want to leave him sometimes, so I could see my friends and go out with Les, stuff like that. Hilary had to be able to feed him then. So she bought me bottles, a sterilizer and a box of disposable nappies. She called it "the starter set". I even had my bag packed for the hospital with some stuff for the baby and my pyjamas, dressing-gown, slippers and toiletries, like it said in one of my pamphlets.

I hadn't picked his name yet, though. I had a book of boys' names that I got in Smiths. I reckoned I'd have plenty of time after I'd had him and knew what he was like to read through it and find the perfect one.

My mother said the doctor could be wrong.

"Is this from all your years of making appointments for other people?" I asked. "Is that what makes you an expert?"

"Don't get clever with me," said my mother. "I have had three children of my own, you know. All I'm saying is you seemed sure about when you stopped bleeding. Maybe the baby *is* small. Some babies are."

"And all I'm saying is what the doctor told *me* yesterday. That he won't be born till September."

"But how do you *feel*?" pushed Detective Spiggs.

How the hell did she think I felt? She was the one who'd had three children of her own. She must've remembered feeling like a hippo with the flu.

"I feel brilliant," I told her. "Never felt better."

"So you don't mind if I spend the night at Charley's? You'll be all right on your own?"

That was her latest torture. She didn't want to leave me because I was so close to my delivery date, in case I was early or something and needed her help. I needed her help like Armani needs Calvin Klein.

"Of course I'll be all right."

She hesitated for a couple of seconds. I could tell she was torn between doing what she thought was right – staying home to torment *me* – and doing what she wanted to do – going to Clapham to torment Charley. She'd never had trouble making this decision before, I can tell you that. She'd been leaving me on my own for as long as I could remember. I reckoned she didn't want the guilt if I died in labour while she was living it up south of the river.

"Well," she said at last. "You have the number if you do need me."

"Burnt into my brain," I said.

It turned out to be a long night.

After the Spiggs went off, I made myself a tin of

soup and a toasted cheese sandwich and curled up on the couch to read about Virgo. I couldn't really get comfortable because my back ached so much. No change there.

I concentrated hard on what the book had to say. It was pretty good news. Virgos are practical and down-to-earth. That sounded all right to me. Shanee was very practical and down-to-earth and I got on fine with her. Also, he'd be adaptable, which wasn't a bad thing. I wondered if I should call him Virgil. Or maybe Vigil. I put them in my mind as definite possibilities.

I had a couple of spoonfuls of soup, but it started repeating almost as soon as I swallowed it. The cheese tasted off. My back was killing me.

I readjusted the pillows and put on a video I'd already seen. I just wanted to hear some human voices, I didn't care what they were saying.

My stomach started to ache. I shuffled into the kitchen and made myself a cup of tea.

It was hard to watch the film at all, because I was so uncomfortable and everything hurt so much.

I started thinking about Les.

He'd been gone four days, but I still hadn't had a postcard. If I'd been Les, I'd've sent me one from the airport, you know sort of as a joke and sort of not as a joke. So I'd know that he missed me like I missed him. But guys aren't the same as girls. It wouldn't even occur to him. Guys live in the present, but girls live in the future. I'd read it in *Cosmo*.

I wondered what Les was doing right then. It was too late for swimming in the sea, but he might be in the pool. Or in the bar with his mates. The bar seemed more likely.

Maybe he was thinking of me.

He was sitting at the bar. I could practically *see* him. Usually Les drank lager, but because he was on holiday he had one of those fancy cocktails with three kinds of spirits, fruit juice, a cherry and a paper parasol stuck in the crushed ice. I'd always dreamed of sitting at a bar, sipping one of those. And Les knew it. He was thinking how much I'd like a drink like that. Since it was Greece, I reckoned there'd be little dishes of olives on the bar as well. And maybe crisps.

Les takes the postcard he bought in the village from his pocket. It's a photograph of a Greek street, like the one Charlene sent me when she went to Greece with her husband. The houses are small and old and painted pink and blue and green. There's a string of onions hanging outside one and a goat sleeping in the shade of a small tree.

Les borrows a pen from the barman and starts to write me a note on the back of the card.

Dear Lana, he writes. *How are you and the baby? How's the weather? It's sunny here, but it might as well be raining. I miss you. You'd really like it here. The hotel's well posh. Carpets and chandeliers, the works. There's a hot tub and a jacuzzi and a whole room of arcade games. Plus, you'd love the food. And there's a disco every night. I was thinking that we might come back here together some time. Like on our honeymoon or something. What do you think?*

I thought the baby was trying to tear his way out of my body, that's what I thought.

A pain ripped through me that was so strong I screamed out loud.

"Jesus," I said to no one.

I didn't want to go to the next thought. The next thought was that something was wrong. Pain like that couldn't be *normal*. I would've heard about it. Madonna would've said something. Or Hilary Spiggs. She wouldn't miss an opportunity like that.

Then the pain stopped. I reckoned that it was just some kind of glitch. You know, the baby got his feet caught in a corner or something like that.

I went back to imagining our honeymoon.

At the disco, Les and I had a spotlit dance to ourselves, because we were newly-weds. He was wearing a white suit, and I was wearing a silver slip dress and silver stilettos. Then, light-headed with love, Les stuck my shoes in his pockets and we linked arms and strolled up the beach beneath a fat, round moon the colour of Flora. Something happy was playing in the background. Maybe ABBA. I'd liked "Dancing Queen" since I saw *Muriel's Wedding*.

Les was telling me how, when he'd been there before, he used to stand at the edge of the water every night and pretend he could see across it to

London. He'd picture me in my black jeans and my sparkly silver top that he liked, going into McDonald's with my shopping.

I screamed again.

It couldn't be the baby kicking, unless he was already wearing boots. Maybe something was wrong. One of the women in the antenatal clinic knew someone whose baby choked to death on the umbilical cord while it was still in the womb. Would it feel like that if it was dying? Would it hurt *me* more than it hurt him?

I sipped my tea and tried to think what to do. I could phone my mother and see what she thought. But it was already after midnight. I didn't want to wake her if it really wasn't anything. I couldn't ring the doctor. I'd only just seen her. She'd think I was being hysterical.

After a while, the pain was coming sort of regularly. Stab ... rest ... stab ... rest ... stab ... rest...

I heaved myself off the sofa and shuffled across the room to get my preggers leaflets.

According to the Going Into Labour section, if what I was feeling *were* contractions, then I should be timing them. Stab ... rest ... stab ... rest...

It would give me something to do besides wince and scream.

I focused on the clock on the video. It was one-thirty in the morning. I couldn't ring Hilary at one-thirty in the morning. Not if it wasn't an emergency.

And it didn't seem to be an emergency. I mean,

it *hurt*, but it didn't hurt that much now I was getting used to it. Plus, I wasn't bleeding or anything. Or only internally.

At two o'clock I gave up timing the contractions. I had no idea what I was timing *for*. Ten minutes apart? Five minutes apart? Three? Then what?

I tried to remember everything I'd ever heard anybody say about having a baby. I knew it was meant to hurt, but hurting was one thing and having your insides pushed out of you was another. I was sure I'd remember that. Mostly what I remembered was what Charlene told me about getting to the hospital and having a needle and not feeling anything more. That I did remember. I could see a woman with a big smile and sweat on her forehead, cradling a newborn infant in her arms. In this image, the newborn infant *was not* holding on to the woman's intestines.

I tried to sleep, but it wasn't any use. It was like trying to fall asleep during a police interrogation.

At two-thirty, I had to go to the loo.

Doubled over, I sort of crept out of the living-room. I was almost afraid to move in case I broke something. Or broke something *else*.

I was taking large, deep breaths, to ease the pain. I almost wished I'd gone to the birthing classes after all, partner or no partner. Then at least I'd know how far apart the contractions had to be before you should call the doctor.

I don't know how I made it to the bathroom. But it didn't matter much, because I didn't make it very far into the bathroom.

I opened the door, but then I just stood there, holding on to the knob.

It was like someone was testing nuclear bombs underground, only I was the ground.

Wham! Something exploded inside me. I was so shocked that I didn't respond until I realized there was water dripping down my legs.

And I knew straight away what was going to happen next. I was going to die there, all by myself, that was what was going to happen. I caught my reflection in the mirror. I was pale and sweating and sopping wet. All I could think was, thank God Les isn't here. I wouldn't want him to see me like this. It was bad enough that the ambulance men who came to take me to the morgue would see me like this.

I burst into tears.

"Oh, my God!"

Even though I was dying a horrible death, I could see what was happening as if I was watching a film.

Les was standing in the doorway. He'd come back because he missed me. No, he'd come back because he had a feeling that I needed him. He'd left his friends sitting by the pool and got the first flight back to London. He was wearing a Greece T-shirt and a straw hat. He dropped the bag and rushed to take me in his arms. "It's all right, darling…" he crooned. "I'm here now…"

But it wasn't Les. It was my mother. She was

standing behind me in a blue woolly hat with a face the colour of a dead fire.

"Lana! I had a feeling—"

"Don't just stand there yammering at me!" I screamed. "*Do something!*"

And then I really started to cry.

Post-Partum Blues

I really loved being on the ward. It was painted pale yellow and the curtains had little bears all over them, so it was really cheerful. There were three other new mothers on the ward with me: Ellen, Anne and Sam, so there was lots going on all the time and lots of chat and laughter. It was almost like a party.

I told the others all about not knowing about the contractions and the doctor telling me I wasn't due and my waters breaking and everything.

Unlike Hilary Spiggs, who'd wanted to know what planet I came from, they all sympathized. And then they told me their own horror stories. It was incredible anybody ever bothered to have a baby really.

Ellen had her second in John Lewis. She called him Lou.

"It was either that or Ladies' Lingerie," she said. "I didn't think Ladies' Lingerie would go down well when he went to school." She laughed. "You have to be careful about names."

I felt like I belonged to a club or something. Except for Anne and me, all the others had had babies before. Ellen had *three*.

"Really?" It was like doing your GCSEs. I couldn't imagine going through it more than once. "You've already got *three* kids?"

"Boys," said Ellen. She grinned. "We wanted a girl."

"I've got two," said Sam. "One of each."

"I don't think I'll have any more," I said.

The others all laughed.

"That's what everybody says," said Sam.

Sam was twenty-four. Next to me, she was the youngest.

She gave me a wink. "You're just a beginner. I was about your age when I started. Trust me, you get used to it."

"Wait till you've had as many as me," said Ellen. "The only thing that scares me is where I'm going to put another one."

Ellen and her husband had a two-bedroom house.

"My parents gave us the deposit as a wedding present," said Ellen. "We've been there longer than you've been alive."

Anne said, "That sounds like heaven to me. Me and Colin moved in with my mum when we got married, and we're still there."

"It's awful living with your mother, isn't it?" I

said. I was feeling really happy now, lying there chatting with everyone like a real woman. Anne was right, I could hardly remember the pain. "Me and my boyfriend are going to get our own flat as soon as we can."

"Lucky you," said Anne. "The only way I'm likely to get away from my mum is if I kill her and they put me in prison."

"Um… Solitary confinement…" said Ellen. "What wouldn't I give…"

"We want something modern," I said. "With a garden for the kids." I'd only just thought of the garden, but I knew exactly what it looked like. It would have a pink Wendy house, just like the one I'd always wanted.

"We wanted a flat of our own," said Anne. "But … well…" She made a face and shrugged. "You don't always get what you want, do you?"

I started to say that you *could* get what you want as long as you didn't give up, but they all shouted at once, "You get what you need!"

I didn't know what they were on about, but I laughed along.

"It's pretty much the same thing, though, isn't it?" I asked when they'd finished shrieking.

Ellen winked. "Not always."

It was like a scene from a movie: me and Hilary Spiggs, shoulder to elbow, staring down at the tiny infant in my arms. Her eyes were closed and she had her fists balled against her mouth. She had this wild punky hair and blotchy skin. There was something sort of froggy about her, but she was still really cute.

"Well, she doesn't look like *you*," said my mother. "She must take after her dad."

This was a leading question. She thought that because I was weak and drowning in hormones I'd finally tell her who the father was. But of course I didn't.

I said, "It's incredible. She has little nails and everything."

It really was incredible. I mean, I *knew* she'd have nails and eyebrows and stuff, but it was still pretty amazing that she did, when you saw them, and how tiny she was.

"What did you expect her to have?" asked my mother. "Claws and fangs?"

Leave it to Hilary Spiggs to ruin any good mood.

I sighed and ran a finger along one of the baby's. It had little knuckles and lines and everything.

"You know what I mean. It's like a magic trick."

"The trick would be getting her to go back," said cheery Nurse Hilary.

I rubbed the tiny knuckles. "I don't want her to go back. I think she's great." Even though she wasn't a boy.

I just hoped Les agreed. I'd sort of thought he'd secretly wanted a son. You know, because he'd never had a brother and his father had died when he was still at primary school. But she did look like him. This could help them bond.

Witch Woman straightened up.

"I told you Charlene can't make it, didn't I?"

I nodded. Charlene's kids both had the flu.

"And Dara's at that conference in Australia."

My sister the international banker. I nodded again.

"But Charley'll come as soon as he's finished work."

I wondered if Les already knew he had a daughter. You know, instinctively.

"That's great."

"So is there anything else you want me to bring when I come back?"

I rubbed some flaky skin from the baby's eyebrow.

"Just my post."

Anne came shuffling over to my bed with a box of chocolates her husband had brought her and her book of baby names. "Haven't you chosen a name yet?"

I looked up from the list I was making. "No. I thought maybe I'd wait to see what she was like."

She sat down on the edge of my bed with a groan. "I swear, the stitches are the worst part." She picked up the pad that was beside me. "What've you got so far?"

"Nothing. The only name that really suits her

is Banshee." She cried so much that they were always taking her out of the ward so she didn't set the others off.

Anne laughed, and Ellen, who was in the bed next to mine, joined in.

Anne flicked through her book. "What about Angelica…? Maia…? Winona…?"

I shook my head. No. No. No.

"What about Cheryl…? Or Amee…? Or Dana…?"

"They just don't seem right."

"Doesn't her dad have any ideas?" asked Ellen.

I laughed. "You know *men*. He wants to name her after his mother."

"And what's that?" asked Anne.

How should I know? The only thing I'd ever heard Les call her was Mum.

"Mary," I guessed.

"It's a little old-fashioned…" said Anne.

"Is he coming tonight?" asked Ellen.

I said, "Who?"

"Your – the baby's dad."

I'd been hoping no one would notice that Les wasn't around. I mean, they all had scads of visitors. Ellen's husband came on his way to work, on his way home from work and after supper with the rest of the kids.

"No," I said quickly. "No. He's away. Working. In Manchester. He can't get back till next week. But he phones me every day. You know, to make sure everything's all right."

"What a shame," said Ellen. "I bet he was upset to miss his daughter's birth."

I nodded. But I didn't want to keep on this subject for too long.

"I just know there's a perfect name floating around somewhere in my mind," I said thoughtfully. "From some film or a song..."

Anne passed the chocolates to Ellen.

"How about Laura?" tried Ellen. "That's from a song."

Not any song I knew.

"Renee," suggested Anne. "That's from a song, too."

I didn't know that one either.

The name situation was actually a little critical. I couldn't get a birth certificate till she had a name. And if I didn't get a birth certificate I would never get my Child Benefit. I was counting on my Child Benefit. Plus, my nan was making a special quilt for the baby. That's what she did, my nan: make quilts. She started when she gave up smoking, so she'd have something to do, and she just kept going. She needed a name before she could finish the quilt. Plus, Les would be back soon. When I finally talked to him I wanted the baby to have a name. So she was real to him. So I could say, "I called her ——. What do you think?"

I bit into my orange cream. "What about Anastasia?"

Anne shook her head. "Too Disney." She poked

136

through the chocolates.

"Martina?"

I liked the sound of the "a" at the end. In my name it made me sound like a bar of soap, but in other names it made them sound foreign and romantic.

"Martina's nice," said Ellen.

"How about Simone?" asked Anne. "I've always liked Simone. It's classy."

"Simona..." I muttered. And then it hit me. Just like that. I snapped my fingers. "I've got it!" I cried. "It's perfect!"

"Well, don't keep us in suspense," urged Ellen. "What is it?"

"Shinola!" I don't know where I heard it, but now that I'd remembered it, I loved it. It was unusual *and* exotic. Shinola Spiggs wasn't brilliant, but Spiggs wouldn't be her last name forever. Soon her name would be Craft. Shinola Craft. Or maybe Shinola Craft-Spiggs. A double-barrelled name can be a help.

Ellen frowned. "Shinola? I don't think I've ever heard that before."

"It almost sounds African," said Anne.

It didn't sound African to me. But it did sound like it would mean something nice like "beautiful morning" or "graceful princess" in whatever language it was.

"Perhaps you should try it out on your boyfriend when he rings."

"Yeah," I said. "That's what I'll do."

My mum and Charley came around seven. They brought me a Big Mac and large fries, an apple pie and a chocolate milkshake. But no postcards except the one from Shanee.

Charley made a fool of himself gurgling at the baby, who decided to take a break from crying to gaze at him blindly. While I ate, the Spiggs yammered on about all the things *I'd* done when *I* was a baby. I was too tired to care. After they left I watched some telly till they turned the lights out.

Everything changed when the lights went out. If the ward was like a party in the day, at night it was like a party after everyone's gone home and left you with the washing-up.

Maybe it was the star balloons Sam's husband brought her that floated over her bed. I'd never thought about being an astronaut or anything like that, but all of a sudden I felt like I was drifting through space all by myself.

Space was cold and scary. It wasn't like in films. There weren't any stations where Han Solo and Chewbacca hung out. Or colonies where a starship might stop. There was just space. I thought about the postcard Hilary didn't bring me from home. What if I never found anywhere to land? What if I just floated like this forever with no one to bring me flowers or balloons?

I almost started crying, but then I had another thought. It wasn't that Les was *ignoring* me. It was that he was *protecting* me. If he had written and

Hilary had seen his card she'd want to know who he was. She'd put two and two together and come up with Dad. Thank God he'd had enough sense to be careful. It made me feel better.

I went back to drifting through space.

There were all sorts of dangers out in space I'd never thought of before. I'd made all sorts of plans for me and the baby. And Les. I knew what our house looked like, and how we'd decorate our Christmas tree – stuff like that. But I hadn't made any plans for what happened if those things didn't happen.

The baby woke up. She was kind of whimpering.

I picked her up how they'd shown me.

"Shhh," I whispered. "You'll wake everyone up."

She stopped whimpering and let out a scream that nearly made me deaf in one ear.

I rang for the nurse.

"It's not really time for another feed," said the nurse. "See if you can get her back to sleep."

I couldn't get her back to sleep. The more I tried, the louder she howled.

The nurse brought a bottle.

The baby didn't want the bottle.

"Well, it's a strange new world to her, isn't it?" said the nurse.

To both of us, I felt like saying.

As soon as the nurse took her, she shut up.

"Maybe she doesn't like me," I whispered.

"Don't be silly." The nurse jiggled my baby in her arms. "Of course she likes you. You're her mum."

"I don't like my mum."

The nurse smiled at Shinola. "You want to go back to mummy now, don't you?"

The baby started howling again.

"You see?" I said. "I told you."

The nurse laughed. "I'll just take her to the nursery. See if I can get her back to sleep."

It was after she disappeared that I got really depressed. Everybody else was sleeping peacefully. Why shouldn't they be? They all had homes with fathers to go back to. When they woke up in the morning their babies' dads would all be there with fruit and messages from their friends and probably a stack of post.

I wished I'd asked Hilary to bring Mr Ted to the hospital. I could've told her it was for the baby. Mr Ted always slept with me, unless Les stayed the night. I really missed him. I sort of bunched up my pillow and pretended I was hugging a bald teddy bear with only one eye, but it wasn't the same.

That's when I started to cry. Just a little at first, but then I really started sobbing. All these thoughts were sort of rushing at my head. There were so many that I didn't know what any of them were. Plus, I didn't want to know. There was something really scary trying to ram itself through my brain. But I wasn't going to let it in.

I tried to sing "Everything's Gonna Be Alright"

in my head but I couldn't. I stopped thinking about anything and just let myself cry.

The nurse came back with the baby, but when she saw the state I was in she took her back to the nursery. Then she brought me a cup of tea.

"Feeling better?" she asked as I sipped.

I nodded.

"Almost everybody gets a little blue after they've had a baby," she told me. "It's the hormones."

"Really?" I snuffled into a tissue. "That's all?"

She fluffed up my pillows.

"That's all," she said cheerfully. She straightened out my blankets. "Once you get home and settled with your baby you'll be as right as rain."

She was one of the older nurses. She was always nice and very calm.

"You think so?"

She took my cup.

"I know so."

I decided to believe her.

Motherhood

Being at home after the hospital was worse than going back to school after the summer holidays; a big disappointment. The Spiggs gave me a couple of days to recover, but after that she made it pretty clear that she expected me to do everything myself.

"I'm not your private nurse, Lana," she informed me. "The party's over. Time to join the real world."

I had no one to talk to like I did on the ward. I couldn't talk to *her* and all my friends were still away. There was no one else around except Mrs Mugurdy. For the first time in my life I was relieved when August finally staggered to an end.

Shanee came over as soon as she got back from Ireland. She brought Shinola some socks, a T-shirt that said "I'm a Full-time Job", and a rubber ducky. She didn't bring anything for me.

"So how's it going?" asked Shanee.

She was standing behind me, watching me change Shinola.

I dodged a small foot that was trying to put out my front teeth.

"It's brilliant," I said. "It really is what life is all about." I pulled Shinola's fist off the nappy tape and sealed her up. "I can't believe there was ever a time when I didn't have her." Which was true in more ways than one; I could hardly go to the toilet without taking her with me.

Shinola went red and rigid at the same time.

"Maybe you did it up too tight," Shanee suggested.

Since it was the first time I'd seen her since Shinola was born, I didn't snap at her the way I would have snapped at Hilary Spiggs.

"It's not too tight," I said, watching the greeny-brown mess that was baby diarrhoea creep out on to her thighs. "She's got the splatters."

Shanee told me all about her holiday while I put another nappy on Shinola. I was too busy clucking and cooing over Shinola to really listen.

Shanee followed me into the kitchen when I went to feed Shinola.

She was still banging on about her holiday and some boy she met who took her for a ride on his motorcycle.

"Wow," I said, juggling Shinola and clucking and cooing. "That sounds cool."

"So," said Shanee. "How's Les?"

I couldn't tell her I hadn't seen Les yet – or even

143

talked to him. I didn't want her to start telling me she told me so or feeling sorry for me.

I swung Shinola so Shanee could get a full view of her. "You should've seen her when she was just born," I said. "She looked like a frog."

"She still looks a bit like a frog," said Shanee.

When Gerri rang I told her that motherhood was brilliant, too.

"You've got to come over and see her," I said. "She's amazing."

Gerri started going on about some boy she'd met at some party.

"It's incredible how fast they grow," I said. "I swear she changes every day."

"I thought it was you who did the changing," said Gerri.

Amie wanted to know about my figure. "Are you doing exercises?" she asked. "Is your stomach still floppy?"

"Wait till you see her," I said. "Yesterday she smiled at me. I know everybody says it's just gas, but she really smiled."

"So what else have you been doing?" asked Amie.

"I've got to go, Amie. Shinola's crying."

"I'm back," said Les. "I'm sorry I didn't ring sooner. I've been busy."

I was so relieved he'd phoned when the Spiggs wasn't home that I didn't even mind that it had taken him a week to get round to it.

144

"Me, too," I said.

Les laughed. "What have you been doing, shopping?"

I laughed, too. "No," I said. "I had the baby. Our baby."

Les said, "What?"

"The baby," I repeated. "I had it. That's what happens after you've been pregnant for nine months," I explained. "You give birth."

"Geez," said Les.

"It's a girl," I said, since he didn't ask. "I called her Shinola."

"Shinola?"

"Yeah. Do you like it?"

"Yeah, it's nice." Les cleared his throat. "What is it, African or something?"

I said I didn't think so. I said it meant sunny morning in Indian or something like that.

"That's great," said Les. "That's really great." I could hear his voice change gear. "I'll ring you later, Lana. I've got to go."

Since I was always tired, I fell asleep at every chance I got, usually in front of the telly. And since Les still hadn't come round, I dreamt about him a lot.

I was dreaming that Les took me and Shinola to Disneyland Paris.

When Charley took me and Hilary to Disney World we stayed with his sister who lives in Florida, but Les got us a room in one of the hotels at the park. Our room was pink and had a white canopy bed and a crystal chandelier. It was the Cinderella suite. Les had booked it specially. There was a little room off the main bedroom for Shinola. It had one of those cradles that rock back and forth like you see in fairy stories, all white net and ruffles and little pink bows.

Shinola was sleeping in her little room and Les and I were getting ready for supper. There was a maid who'd look after Shinola while we went downstairs to eat so we didn't have to stay in our room. After dinner we were going to the disco.

The hotel radio station was playing songs from great Disney classics while I got into my party gear. "Someday My Prince Will Come" was on.

I zipped up my dress. It was a red dress with a tight bodice and spaghetti straps and a slightly flared skirt. I had red heels to match. I sat down at the white and gold dressing-table to put on my make-up. It was just like the dressing-table I'd always wanted (but *she* would never let me have), with lights around the mirror. Les came up behind me. He started nuzzling my neck and telling me how gorgeous I looked. I pretended I didn't want him messing up my hair and stuff, but really I couldn't have cared less.

"Lana…" whispered Les. "Lana … Lana … Lana…"

He was being too rough. I pushed him off.

"Lana … Lana … Lana…"

"Not now." I pushed him off again. "I have to get ready."

"Lana … Lana … Lana…" He wasn't nuzzling me any more. He was shaking me hard.

I pulled away from him. "Get dressed," I said. "You've got to get dressed, too."

"Not at three in the morning," said Les.

I opened my eyes. I'd fallen asleep in front of the telly again. But even though I was still half-asleep and blinded I knew it wasn't Les's come-to-bed eyes that were staring down at me. I shut my own tight.

"Lana, wake up."

I risked another look. Hilary was standing over me with no make-up on and her hair in curlers like some monster of the night. I wanted to hit her.

"What do you want?"

"What do *I* want? Can't you hear Shinola? She's been crying for ten minutes."

Then why didn't she look after her, for God's sake? I pulled a cushion over my head. "So give her a bottle."

She threw the cushion on to the floor. "I'm not her mother. She needs you, Lana. *Now*."

There was nothing for it, she was going to get me up if she had to drag me off the couch. I sat up, rubbing my eyes.

"I can't have my sleep disturbed like this every night," she complained. "I've got to go to work."

She'd taken a week off after I got home from hospital, to look after me and Shinola, and that was hell. But this was worse. Before she complained all the time, but at least she got up with Shinola in the

147

night once in a while and made a few bottles. Now all she did was complain.

"All right ... all right..." I got to my feet and staggered into the kitchen.

"Pick Shinola up before you heat the bottle," she nagged. "She's upset. She needs to be comforted."

"I'll comfort her once I've done this," I said, though at that moment I'd sooner have stuffed her down the loo. "I've only got two hands."

There were three bottles ready in the fridge, thank God. I wasn't up to any major preparation. Not with the Curse of Kilburn shrieking at me.

"Heat the water first," ordered my mother. "You don't want it hot, you just want it warmed."

I put a bottle in a cold pan of water and turned on the burner. "I know how hot to make it," I informed her. "I *have* done this before."

She didn't say anything. I glanced over my shoulder to see why. You know, to see if she was putting a curse on me or something and couldn't be bothered to answer. She was gone.

Though not for long.

She came back before I had time to miss her, Shinola squirming in her arms.

"Look at her!" she said accusingly. "She's almost blue."

She was closer to purple than blue, if you asked me.

"And that's *my* fault?" I screamed back. "Even though I didn't hear her?"

148

Some things never changed. I still got blamed for everything, but now she had more things to blame me for.

"You *should've* heard her," snarled my mother. "Either you bring her cot into the living-room, or you take the telly into your room."

But when she talked to Shinola she was as sweet as pie. "There ... there..." she crooned. "Your bottle will be ready in a minute. There ... there ... there..."

I took Shinola out of her arms. "She'll puke if you keep jiggling her like that."

"No, she won't," said my mother. "She has nothing in her *to* puke."

It was another week before Les could come over – because of work and having to catch up after his holiday and everything. He had a surprise for me. "I can't wait to see your face when you see it," said Les.

It'd been so long since anyone had given *me* anything that wasn't really for Shinola that I instantly forgave him for not coming round sooner.

I spent the whole day getting ready.

Les was a very neat person. I didn't want him to think that motherhood had made me sloppy, so I tidied the flat up first. It took ages because every time I'd get stuck into the washing-up or something, Shinola would start screaming.

Then I gave her a bath and changed her so she wouldn't smell like something that'd gone off. As soon as I snapped the last snap on her rompers, she did the biggest dump anyone smaller than an elephant could possibly do. I had to start all over again.

I hadn't even finished doing my make-up when the doorbell rang.

Shinola was whingeing, of course, so I scooped her up and raced to the door.

Les looked surprised. "Jesus Christ," he said.

I smiled down at her. "Say hello to your father." I waved her little hand at him. It was wet with drool.

Les had half a smile on his face. Not a small smile, but half a smile, as if only one half of his mouth could actually move. He kind of shuffled from one foot to the other, his eyes on Shinola. I'd been hoping he'd be choked with emotion the first time he saw her, but he wasn't, unless the emotion was nervousness.

"She's sweet," said Les. "She looks like you."

I pretended to study Shinola's face as though I'd never looked at it before, when really it was just about all I did look at any more.

"You think so? I think she's got your nose."

Les laughed. "She hasn't got anybody's nose. She's got her own."

He stood there, nodding and grinning, his eyes on Shinola as if he thought she was a letter-bomb.

"So," I said. "Do you want some tea? Tell me all about your holiday."

Les threw himself on to the sofa beside a box of disposable nappies. The sofa honked. Startled, he reached behind him and removed a blue rubber duck.

"I can't imagine what it's going to be like when she can walk," I said. "Her stuff gets everywhere as it is."

Les's nose twitched. "She hasn't done something, has she? It smells funny in here."

"Of course not." There was no way I was going to start changing nappies then. It was the first time we'd been together in weeks. I wanted Les to think of me as his sex goddess, not the girl with the poo-smeared cotton ball in her hand. "Why don't I put the kettle on while you tell me about your holiday?"

Les leaned back with a sigh. "Don't let me bang on too long," he said. "I'm becoming a bit of a Greece bore." He laughed. "You're lucky I forgot my snaps."

Shinola'd only been whimpering, you know, so we wouldn't forget she was there. But as soon as Les started to talk about his holiday, she started to cry for real.

"Shhh, shhh..." I whispered. "Daddy's trying to tell us something."

"It was the most brilliant time I've ever had," Les was saying. He raised his voice to be heard over Shinola. "I went swimming every day. And I went fishing a couple of times and even scuba-diving. I really—"

I turned from the sink, holding the baby with one hand and the kettle with the other. "What?" I shouted. "Swimming, fishing and what?"

"Scuba-diving!" roared Les. "I really liked the scuba-diving. But it's not as easy as you think."

I'd never thought about scuba-diving at all and I wasn't about to start just then. Les yammered on about scuba-diving and all the things you have to learn so you don't kill yourself or anything, but there was no way I could really hear him. Not with trying to get the tea things out and Shinola shrieking in my ear. I didn't want to interrupt him every three words to say "What?" Plus, I didn't really care. He might as well have been talking about star surfing, it seemed so foreign and far away.

I came back into the living-room while he was going on about the fishing. He hadn't caught anything.

"What a shame," I said. "Still, you got a good tan."

Les beamed. "And no sunburn. Usually I burn badly, but this time my nose didn't even peel."

I moved the nappies and put Shinola on the sofa beside him to bond. She'd settled down a bit once the tea was made, but as soon as she hit the couch she started up again.

Les jumped to his feet. "Christ!" He slapped his forehead. "Your surprise! How could I forget?"

It was a T-shirt that said "Winner of the Wet T-shirt Competition, Sunnytime Holidays" and then something in what I reckoned must be Greek.

At least it was Greek to me.

"Try it on," shouted Les.

"But the tea—"

He winked. "The tea can wait." He winked again. "You have to wear it without a bra."

I had to go in the kitchen to take my bra off because people could see into the living-room from the street. Les came after me.

I stuck out my chest. "How does it look?"

Les grinned. "It looks better when it's wet, but it looks pretty good."

I looked down. "They're not so big any more."

"They're big enough for me," said Les.

The way he said it made me feel all tingly.

Les took a step towards me.

I took a step towards him.

Our lips touched.

Shinola really started to scream.

Les jumped back as though my mouth was hot.

"Christ," he said. He glanced at his watch. "I'd better get going. I can't be late. Not after being on holiday."

I tried to hide my disappointment. "But we haven't had our tea! You must have time for tea."

Les shook his head. "I really have to go." He touched my breast. "And anyway, it's really hard to concentrate with her screaming like that."

I followed him to the front door.

"When am I going to see you again?"

153

"Soon. I'll drop by."

"Maybe we could have lunch one day."

"Yeah," said Les. "That'd be great. I'll ring you, OK?"

I said, "OK."

Shinola shrieked. If she was a car alarm someone would've smashed the windscreen by now.

Shinola was still screaming when the doctor's receptionist from hell came home.

"What on earth have you been doing to this baby?" she demanded.

She grabbed her out of my arms. As per usual, she was all sweet and soft and coocoocoo with Shinola. But not with me.

"What were you doing to let her get in this state?" she demanded. She looked me up and down. "Putting on make-up?"

She said it like it was a crime or something.

"No," I said. "I put it on before. Anyway, the book says it's all right to let her cry."

She rocked Shinola back and forth in her arms.

"Maybe you should get another book," said my mother.

I was beginning to think they'd forgotten about me, but Shanee, Gerri and Amie finally found some time in their busy lives to pay me a visit.

I was really warming to my story. I'd had all the other mothers in the maternity ward and the nurses and everyone to tell about my experience, but this was the first time I'd told the story of

Shinola's birth to any of my friends. It was having a powerful effect.

"Oh, my God..." screeched Gerri. "Weren't you terrified?"

"I can't believe I wasn't here when you needed me," said Shanee. "Poor Lana."

Amie held up her hands. "Please," she begged, "I've heard enough. I'm never having children unless I can have a Caesarean."

"That hurts too," said Shanee.

"It can't be as bad as what Lana went through," said Amie. She shuddered. "I can't even think of it without feeling sick."

I laughed. I was enjoying myself. I felt really grown up, telling them all about giving birth and stuff. At last I knew something none of them knew.

"It wasn't all that bad, really," I said. "I mean, you know you're not dying or anything. And, besides, you forget about it as soon as you see your baby."

"Speaking of your baby, when do we see her?" asked Gerri.

I glanced at the clock. Babies are meant to follow a routine – sleep, eat, get changed, go back to sleep – but Shinola liked to leave out as much of the sleep bit as she could. She usually finally passed out round about the time she should've been waking up again.

"I put her to bed just before you came. She won't be up for at least an hour."

"We don't have that long," said Shanee. "I've got to get back to mind the brats."

"Can't we just take a peek?" asked Gerri.

I'd've preferred to have time to dress Shinola up in one of her cute little dresses, you know, so she looked less froggy. On the other hand, I did want to show her off.

"All right," I said. "But you have to be quiet."

We tiptoed into the bedroom and all stood round Shinola's cot. She looked really sweet in her yellow sleep bag.

"What's wrong with her skin?" asked Gerri.

"Nothing," I whispered. "All babies look like that."

"Do they all have hair like that, too?" asked Amie. "And flaky eyebrows?"

"For God's sake!" I hissed at her. "She's only just been born. Give her a chance."

"So does she look like Les?" asked Amie.

"I think she looks like Lana," said Shanee.

"She looks like Les," I assured them. "Except she's not so tall."

"What did he say when he saw her?" asked Gerri.

It was always Gerri with the big mouth.

"He was delirious." Which I was sure he would be. Eventually. "He came over as soon as he got back from Manchester."

I didn't want them thinking Les wasn't so interested in me, so I'd told them he'd been sent up to Manchester with his job. It sounded better than him going on holiday to Greece.

"Where was your mum?" asked Gerri. "Don't tell me they've finally met!"

I gave her a look. "Not likely. She still doesn't know about him." I gave her another look. "And she's not going to. Not yet."

"That's going to make conjugal visits a little dodgy, isn't it?" asked Gerri.

"Come on." I grabbed hold of her and Amie and tugged. "Let's go back to the living-room. We're going to wake her up."

They'd all been oohing and aahing right over the cot, and we'd had a whole conversation right over her head, but it was the really soft shutting of the bedroom door that woke her. Click went the door and the next sound was Shinola Spiggs going off like a car alarm.

"Geez," said Gerri. "Is there a pin in her or something?"

I rolled my eyes. "Pampers don't have *pins*. She must've heard the door and it woke her up."

"Does she always scream like that?" asked Amie.

"Do you want me to get her?" asked Shanee.

"She'll be all right. I'll put on some music, it'll help her sleep."

I put on an Oasis CD and made us all some tea.

Gerri started telling me about her new boyfriend. He was a bicycle courier and had a terrific body. Plus, he was gorgeous. Plus, he made good money.

Shinola kept crying, but the Gallaghers' whining was pretty good at blocking her out. You could only just hear her under the music. Shanee glanced towards the hallway a few times, but I pretended I thought Shinola had gone back to sleep and Shanee didn't say anything.

I started really enjoying myself again. Only now I didn't feel grown up, like when I talked about having Shinola. I just felt like me.

Amie had a part-time job in one of the pizza places on the high street. The boss was a miserable old git, but the tips weren't bad.

Shinola kept crying.

Shanee stood up suddenly. "I think we'd better get going." She looked towards the hall.

"You don't have to go so soon," I said. I grabbed the pot from the table. "Why don't I make us all more tea?"

Gerri and Amie both looked at Shanee.

"I've got stuff to do, too," said Gerri.

Amie winked. "And I'm expecting an important call."

That meant a boy.

I had to stop myself from shoving her back in her seat. "He'll call back," I insisted. "Just have another cup of tea."

"Next time," said Gerri.

Amie nodded. "Yeah, next time, Lana."

"Why don't you go and get the baby," said Shanee. "We can let ourselves out."

I watched the three of them leave the house from

the front window. They didn't even look back to wave goodbye. They were laughing and talking as though they couldn't hear Shinola from the road. I knew that they could from the times that I'd left her to ring Les from the phone box so Hilary wouldn't see the number on the phone bill. You could hear her from the high street.

I watched them all go off towards Shanee's and I wondered if there would ever be a next time. And then, instead of going to Shinola, I burst into tears myself.

A Job for Life

Although Les came round every couple of days before work, he was so busy after being on holiday that it was October before we finally managed to have lunch.

It wasn't the best day to take Shinola out. I knew that. It was really cold for October and it was pouring down. But I wasn't going to let a bit of bad weather put me off seeing Les.

Plus, I was really bored of being at home on my own all the time. Shanee was always busy with school and stuff, and, when she did come round, Shinola was always up and squawking so we could never really talk. Amie and Gerri never bothered coming round after that first time at all. They had more important things to do.

Anyway, I was so busy with everything else I had to do that I hadn't made any more bottles after Shinola had her breakfast. Plus, I wanted her to wear the red and blue tartan dress Shanee gave her, but the tartan dress was still in the laundry from the last time she wore it. So, because of having to make her a couple of bottles, and wash and dry the dress, it took ages to get us ready.

As I was running late, I had to put my eye make-up on with one hand while I held Shinola on my hip with the other. She squirmed and gurgled so much that I ended up with one eye that looked naked and one eye that looked like someone'd punched me, and tears in both. I wiped off as much of the extra as I could.

"It'll have to do," I said to our reflection in the mirror. We didn't look like the pictures I'd seen of Madonna and her baby, that's for sure. We looked more like one of those advertisements in the paper asking for money to help kids in the Third World.

I sprayed some Tommy Girl on me and a tiny bit on Shinola. Even if we didn't *look* like a trendy mother and daughter we could smell like them.

Shinola didn't like the perfume.

I hoped she wasn't going to turn out to be a tomboy. I looked down at her. She didn't look very feminine. In fact, she looked sort of like a boy. What if she turned out to be a lesbian? I hadn't thought about that.

I almost forgot about Les and lunch for a couple of minutes while I started worrying about all the things Shinola could turn out to be that I hadn't thought of. I was starting to realize that having a kid wasn't like buying a dress. When you bought a dress you knew what you'd bought: a dress. If you got home and realized it wasn't a dress you would actually want to be seen in, alive *or* dead, you could take it back. But when you had a baby you didn't really know what you'd got. Shinola drooled down my sweater. And you couldn't take it back.

I put on another sweater and some more Tommy Girl. By now I was going to be lucky to get to McDonald's on time, even if we had a helicopter. I threw a couple of nappies and a bottle into Shinola's bag, stuck her in her buggy, and raced out of the house.

Catching a bus with a baby is about as much fun as catching a bus with a temperamental ostrich under your arm. I tried to take Shinola out every day if I could, so we were used to buses by now, but this was our first bus trip in the rain. Which meant we had more gear than usual. You never go *anywhere* with a baby without lugging enough stuff to go camping for a week.

To get on the bus, I had to take Shinola out of her buggy and fold it up. To get her out of her buggy, I had to remove her from the plastic bubble. Then, with one hand, I had to fold up the push-chair. Only it wouldn't fold flat with the plastic bubble inside, and I couldn't get it locked in place. Then I had to get Shinola and me and the buggy on to the bus. Nobody offered to help, not even when the damn thing sprang open and nearly pulled us back to the pavement.

It was one of those little single-decker buses, and because it was raining, it was packed. So once you got up the stairs there wasn't actually anywhere to go.

"Seventy pence," said the driver.

I didn't have my money ready, and I couldn't get it out because I only had two hands, and one of them was trying to hold the buggy shut and the other was trying to hold Shinola.

"Could you wait till I put the pushchair away?"

"Seventy pence," said the driver.

As per usual, Shinola started to cry. I could feel everybody capable of even the slightest movement turn to look at us.

"For God's sake," I hissed at her. "Not *now*!"

But would she listen? Sometimes I worried that she was going to be like her grandmother.

By sort of wedging the buggy between me and the driver, I managed to fish the change from my pocket.

"Move back!" shouted the driver. "Everybody move back!"

I stuck the ticket between my teeth and tried to move back.

It was like trying to get a motorbike through a tin of sardines.

The luggage rack was full.

"Move back! Move back!"

As though she was joining in with the driver, Shinola was wailing, "Wahwah... Wahwah..."

I forced my way towards the back, saying "Excuse me," and "Pardon me," every time I whacked somebody with the buggy.

An old lady finally gave me her seat.

"Sounds like he might have a touch of the colic," she said as we exchanged places.

"*She*," I corrected. "But I don't think it's colic."

I had no idea what colic was. It's one of those words that everybody uses but no one ever tells you what it means. Plus, I really didn't think it was anything like that. I was beginning to think she did it on purpose.

The old lady beamed down on us. "Isn't he sweet? I remember when mine were that age." She beamed again. "Enjoy it while it lasts," she told me. "The time goes very quickly."

Not quickly enough, if you asked me.

We were late, but Les was later. I reckoned he must've been held up in traffic.

Shinola and I stood in the doorway, waiting. The traffic was really noisy because it was standing still, and the rain was still falling by the bathfull, so naturally Shinola fell asleep. I pictured Les running down the street to us, trying to get through the shoppers with their umbrellas and trolleys as quickly as he could. He was worried that we'd been waiting so long. He was anxious to see us. And then, from the end of the road, he would see us. That song from the BT ad started playing in the background, "Oh, What a Perfect Day", or something like that. His face lit up. "Lana!" he shouted. "Lana! I'm here!" He practically scooped the two of us up in his arms, buggy and all...

After a while, I thought maybe we'd be better off inside. Shinola was all right because she was under the plastic bubble, but *I* was getting soaked. I felt like I was wearing sponges on my feet.

Les was sitting in a corner. I spotted him straight away. He'd already started eating.

"Les!" I waved. "Les!"

He looked up and shook his burger in our direction.

"I thought you weren't coming," he said when we finally made it to his table. He nodded at the window. "Because of the weather." He wasn't going to stand outside waiting in the rain. That's how you caught cold.

Shinola woke up while Les was getting me my lunch. She blinked at the lights and stuck a fist in her mouth, which pretty much amounted to Shinola's party trick.

I took her out of the buggy and laid her on my lap. She was being really good. She was awake, but she was gurgling.

Les looked over at her as he sat back down. He reached out a finger and kind of rubbed her chin. I'm sure he didn't say "Gicheegicheegoo", but he said something that sounded a lot like "Gicheegicheegoo". Shinola showed him her gums.

"She really does look like you," said Les. He said

165

whatever it was he was saying to her again. Shinola bubbled. At least she was bonding all right.

Les started telling me what was happening at work.

It was spite, I knew it was. She couldn't stand not having *everybody's* attention, *all* the time.

Shinola started to howl.

Les glanced nervously around us.

"Can't you shut her up?" he hissed. "Everybody's looking at us like we're trying to murder her."

As far as one of us was concerned, Shinola was lucky someone wasn't trying to murder her.

I smiled, calm and controlled, a proper mother.

"She must be hungry. I've got a bottle in her bag."

"Thank God for that," breathed Les.

But I didn't have her bag.

I looked under the table three times, but it wasn't there.

I groaned. "I must've left it on the bus."

"You should've left *her* on the bus," joked Les.

People really were looking at us like we were sticking hot knives in her.

"Can't you take her to the ladies and feed her?" he pleaded.

I always tried not to tell Les the same thing twice, so I didn't bore him, but I forgot about that rule now.

"I don't have a bottle," I said again. "I left her bag on the bus."

166

Les looked at his watch. "I'm going to have to go. I've got to get to work."

"But I thought you didn't have to be there till four."

"Albie called in sick," said Les. "I've got to be in by two."

He already had his jacket on.

I knew it wasn't cool, but I couldn't help it.

"But when am I going to see you properly? I miss you, Les. It's been so long."

His eyes sort of shuffled. "I'll stop by when I can, Lana, but I can't do more than that right now." He snapped his fingers. "Hey, what about your birthday? Isn't that coming up? See if you can get someone to look after her, and we'll go out. See a film or something. Have a meal." He winked. "Celebrate."

Happiness flooded through me. He'd remembered my birthday. And he wanted to have a proper date. Everything was all right.

"That'd be great. I haven't been to the cinema in ages. I'll tell the Spiggs I'm going with Shanee."

"I'll ring you," said Les. "You pick the day."

You never think about it when you watch a film, but most of the time the characters in films have a lot of luck. It may seem like they're just getting the destiny they deserve because they're doing what they know is right or whatever, but actually it's luck.

I knew that because I didn't have any luck.

167

Unless you were counting bad luck.

Something went wrong with the boiler at the doctor's where my mother worked and everyone was sent home in case it exploded or something.

I saw her at the window as me and Shinola the Screamer came up the path. She was on the phone. I saw relief in her face for just a second, and then I saw rage.

Oh, no, I thought. Not now...

She slammed the phone down and was in the hall before I'd got the buggy inside.

"Where the hell have you been?" she screeched. "How could you take her out on a day like this?"

"For God's sake," I yelled back. "People live in igloos. A little rain's not going to hurt her."

She scooped Shinola out of the buggy and disappeared back into the living-room.

I shook out the buggy, and me, and hung my jacket on a hook in the hall.

She was still screeching even though I wasn't in the room with her.

I didn't really listen. I'd heard it all before.

"Blahblahblah infection ... blahblahblah death of cold ... blahblahblah trauma and exhaustion ... blahblahblah."

I went straight to my room to change out of my sopping wet things.

By the time I got to the kitchen, she already had a bottle in Shinola's mouth.

"She's starving." She gave me the same look Mrs Mela used to give me when I didn't do my homework. "Didn't you feed her this afternoon?"

Shinola wasn't the only one who was starving. After Les left I didn't even stay to have my lunch. There didn't seem any point – especially with her in the state she was in. I took a packet of biscuits from the cupboard and put the kettle on.

"Of course I fed her," I lied. "She just never gets enough."

My mother gave me a look about as sweet as a pint of vinegar, then turned back to the baby.

"Where's poor little Nola been?" she cooed, all mushy and gooey. "Where did Lana take you?"

"Her name's Shinola, not Nola." I thumped the milk carton down on the counter. "And I took her out for some fresh air."

"In a storm," said the caring grandmother. She kissed the top of Shinola's head. "Did Lana take you out in the storm? Did she forget to feed you?"

I slammed the sugar down. "I didn't forget anything!" I roared. "For the hundredth time, I told you, I fed her."

"As soon as you finish your bottle, we'll put you into some nice warm jammys."

I had to stop myself from throwing the tea caddy at her.

"She isn't wet!" I screamed. "I'm the one who got soaked to the skin."

"Who takes a newborn baby out in a hurricane?"

If there'd been a few snow flurries it would've been a blizzard.

"I do, that's who!"

"And what does that prove?" Hilary Spiggs demanded. "The only baby you've ever handled in your life is yourself."

"I'm her mother, not you!" I took Shinola from her so quickly she was too surprised to stop me. "And you can just mind your own bloody business."

She squashed her lips together and looked at me for a few seconds.

"You'd better watch yourself, young lady," said the Mother of the Year. "Or I may just do that."

I told her Shanee wanted to take me out for my birthday.

To my surprise she didn't even put up a fight.

"That sounds like a good idea," she said. "You don't see enough of your friends. Just tell me what night and I'll make sure I have no plans."

Saturday was my birthday, but Les had to work on Saturday.

"Friday," I said. "That's the only night Shanee can do it."

"Friday it is, then," said my mother.

Being so nice and smarmy wasn't like my mother at all. She had to be up to something. And I was pretty sure I knew what it was. Once I was sixteen, I was applying for my own council flat. Even though she said she couldn't wait to get rid of me, I reckoned she didn't want me to go. Then she'd *have* to admit I was an adult. And then she'd have to treat me like one. For a change. So she was going to try and make herself useful. So I'd want to stay. She had as much chance of that happening as she did of winning an Oscar.

Because the Spiggs threw in looking after Shinola while I got ready, I was not only able to have a real bath for the first time since Shinola was born, but I was standing in front of the cinema at exactly seven, cool and sophisticated in a silver slip dress and the double-breasted, three-quarter-length coat I bought in the market with my birthday money. A couple of guys gave me the eye while I was waiting, but I pretended I didn't notice.

At exactly seven-thirty, when the programme was meant to start, I began to get worried. Maybe Les'd had an accident. These things happened all the time. Mrs Wallace, my teacher in Year Nine, had lost her husband because he'd been crossing a zebra at the same time as a car. He'd gone out for some milk and never came back. That could've happened to Les. Or a joy rider could've ploughed into his car. That had happened in one of my favourite soaps.

He turned up at a few minutes past eight.

"You wouldn't believe the traffic," he told me. "It wasn't just slow, it was parked."

"It's not your fault," I assured him. "But we missed the film."

Les must've heard the disappointment in my voice. He gave me a hug.

171

"I'm sorry," he said. "I really am." He kissed my forehead. "You look great."

This was exactly the sort of thing I wanted to hear.

Les grinned as if he'd just had the best idea since Coca-Cola.

"Tell you what. Why don't we get a takeaway and go back to mine? They're all away for the weekend. There's a good film on the telly. We can watch that instead." He rubbed his head against mine. "Be comfortable."

I'd sort of thought we'd go to McDonald's, you know, since it was our anniversary as well, but this was better. This was beyond my wildest dreams. Really. Les's flatmates never seemed to go anywhere, except at Christmas. The house to ourselves! We could watch telly in bed, just like married people do.

"OK," I said. "That sounds good to me."

Riding back to Dollis Hill, I felt like Princess Diana must've felt riding in her limo to the palace. You know, before everything went so wrong between her and Prince Charles. I felt that chuffed. I looked out of the car window, watching the gangs of girls hanging out together on a Friday night, and they looked like little kids dressed up for a party.

Not me. I had a baby at home being looked after by her nan, and I was spending the night with my man. Mrs Mela could take her *Romeo and Juliet* and stuff it. This was almost as perfect as anything could get.

Les had my present all ready. It was wrapped and everything.

"Oh, wow," I said. "Another charm."

This one was a gold baby bottle. Personally, I'd still have preferred a heart.

"It seemed to suit you," said Les.

I thanked him with a kiss.

He kissed me back.

"Come on upstairs," he said, kissing me and pulling me at the same time.

Later, after we'd had our takeaway and officially given up on the film and discovered that one of Les's flatmates must have taken the condoms he'd finally bought, he wrapped his arms around me with his head on my shoulder.

"Isn't this better? Just the two of us?" he whispered.

I snuggled against him. I could see us getting up in the morning and brushing our teeth side by side at the sink.

"I wish it could always be like this," I whispered back.

A little later he said, "So, are you going to stay the night?"

That was the first time I'd thought about going home. I was so happy, I'd lost track of everything. Including the time. But I resisted the urge to bolt out of bed and start putting on my clothes. He'd never invited me to spend the night at his place before. How could I say "No"?

"I really should get back..." I said.

"What difference does a couple more hours make?" asked Les. "It's not as if your mum's got somewhere to go. You can always tell her you went to what's her name's."

"Shanee's."

"To Shanee's."

I couldn't really think straight because he started kissing me again.

"Well…" I said. "I suppose I could stay just a little longer…"

She was right there in the hall, waiting for me when I finally got home. She had her arms folded in front of her. She looked like she'd been stuffed in a moment of anguish. Like the bear we saw at the museum in primary school. Only with a pink scarf tied around her head over her curlers.

"I'm sorry," I said, before she could say anything. "Shanee and I went for a coffee after the film." I casually squeezed past her. "God, I'm tired."

"You drank coffee till nearly five in the morning?" asked my mother.

I took off my jacket. "We were having such a good time that we went back to hers. Since it's the weekend." I hung my jacket on a hook. "It was really great. I haven't had a chance to really talk to Shanee in *ages*." I gave her a smile. "Thanks." I turned towards my room.

"Not so fast," said Gruppenführer Spiggs. "I rang Shanee's at midnight. Her mother said

Shanee'd been home for nearly an hour. *Alone.*"

I laughed. "You know Mrs Tyler. There are so many people in and out she never knows *who's* there."

Hilary Spiggs snorted like the old hog she was. "Well, *you* weren't."

I looked her in her beady eyes. "Yes, I was."

"No, you weren't. Lucy went and checked. Shanee was sound asleep."

"All right, all right ... I ran into some friends I hadn't seen in ages, and I went with them. Shanee didn't want to come."

She smiled. "Oh, really?"

I kept looking at her, but I got ready to make a quick retreat.

"Really."

"And might one ask why you've got your dress on inside out?"

I went numb for a second. I didn't have to look down, though, to know that she was right. I could feel the seam of my dress with my hand.

"It's not inside out. It's meant to be this way." I said it like I thought she'd lost her mind.

And then she did.

She knew where I was. I was out with *him*. Wasn't one baby enough for me? Did I want more? Couldn't I see that he was only using me?

That was when *I* lost it. "You don't know anything about it!" I screamed. "We happen to be in love."

"Love?" she screamed back. "You think this is

love? If he really loved you he'd do more than take you to bed when he fancies."

"Shut up!" I wanted to shake her. "Shut up and mind your own business for a change."

She went dead calm. "Fine," said my mother. "I'll mind my own business. Because I'll tell you one thing, Miss All-grown-up: I'm not going to mind your brats while you tart yourself around town. If you want to play house, you can play house on your own. I'm moving down to Charley's for a while. You're sixteen now. Sort yourself out and then you're on your own. I'll leave you housekeeping money in the blue teapot and I'll talk to you in a couple of days." She looked like she wanted to shake me. "Don't ring me; I'll ring you," and then she banged past me and into her room.

Shinola started crying the second the door slammed shut.

Home Alone

When she lived with us, Hilary made me get up when she got up for work, even if I'd been awake half the night with Shinola. She said it was so she could see I had a proper breakfast, but I knew it was just to torment me and make me suffer like her. If she had to get up at seven, then I had to, too. The first thing she'd do when she got back from work was check to see that I'd done everything she thought I should've done in the day. "Did you do the washing... Did you tidy your room... Did you do the washing-up?" Nagnagnag. Supper was at seven-thirty, unless I hadn't got round to starting it, when it was more like eight. Tea and biscuits were at ten, bed at eleven. Which is another example of how much living with Hilary Spiggs was like being in prison.

But now she'd gone I didn't have to live by *her* schedule. Except for being on twenty-four hour call for Shinola, there was nothing I *had* to do at

177

or by a certain time. I could have cereal for supper or eat breakfast at noon if I wanted. I could stay up watching telly till it shut down. I could fall asleep on the couch. I could do the housework when I felt like it. I could do as I pleased.

Which wasn't all that much. We'd watch the morning kids' programmes, and then we'd go out if it wasn't raining too hard – down to the shops or the post office or whatever – and then the rest of the day we just mooched around. I always had either the telly or the radio on, just so I could hear adult voices. When Shinola had her afternoon nap, since I had nothing else to do that wasn't a chore, I had one, too.

The ringing of the doorbell finally woke me up. The room was dark. I reckoned it must be Shanee on her way home.

I started to sit up, but Shinola kind of grunted and shifted.

I didn't want her to wake up. I wanted Shanee to myself for a change. The last time I saw her I hadn't heard anything she was saying, I was so busy with Shinola.

Very, very slowly and carefully, I rolled myself off the bed. Once I was safely on the floor I peered over the mattress. Her eyelids were kind of twitching but she wasn't crying. Which meant she was still asleep.

Holding my breath, I crawled towards the door, keeping as low to the carpet as I could. When I was hidden behind Shinola's cot I stopped. The door, thank God, was open. I took a deep breath and made a dash for it.

Shanee nearly knocked me over getting into the hall.

"For God's sake, Lana. What took you so long? I thought I was going to drown out there."

"Shh," I whispered. "She'll hear you."

Shanee looked puzzled. "You mean Hilary's back?"

"Not her. Shinola."

"Oh," said Shanee, and she tiptoed into the kitchen behind me.

"I did come round yesterday," she said as I shut the hall door. She dumped her bag and her wet jacket on a chair. "But you never answered."

"Babies really take up a lot of time," I replied. "It's not like school. You don't get a lunch break. I must've been busy and didn't hear you. Unless I was out."

"Or sleeping," said Shanee.

I didn't like her tone.

"What's that mean?"

"It doesn't mean anything. I was only joking. You just never seem to be around when I call." She removed a pile of stuff from another chair and sat down.

"Babies are also very exhausting," I said. "It's like being on guard duty twenty-four hours a day."

"Well, you're not doing such a brilliant job of

179

guarding it," she said. "The place looks like it's been bombed."

I glanced around. It had looked a little like something in a magazine when I'd finished de-Hilarizing it, but that was weeks ago. Shanee was right. Now it looked like something in a war zone.

"That's Shinola," I said. "I never get to finish putting anything away."

"Speaking of work," said Shanee. "Guess what? I got a part-time job!"

"Do you want tea?" I was already filling a pan with water.

"What happened to the kettle?" asked Shanee.

I shrugged. "It broke." It burnt itself to a crisp. "You know Hilary, she only buys cheap junk."

"And what about her nice blue teapot? Don't tell me that broke, too."

"Yeah," I said. It broke when I threw it across the room. It was either the teapot or Shinola. "Everything's breaking."

"So, anyway," said Shanee. "I got this part-time job!"

I told her that was brilliant.

"I know." She hugged herself. "I am sooo excited. I'm working at that new gift shop with all the candles and the inflatable vases and stuff. They've taken me on for Christmas, but if I do OK I can probably have it for good."

"I've got an appointment with the housing next week," I said. "That's pretty quick."

Shanee nodded. "That is quick." Without stopping for breath she went on, "It was such a piece of luck. There was a sign in the window so I got all my courage up and went in and asked. The woman said I had the right look."

"You mean second-hand clothes and hair like a squirrel's nest?"

Shanee laughed. "Fashion's catching up with me. Black and purple and your cousin's old motor-cycle boots are considered very *in* this season."

Shinola had made it through the doorbell, but the sound of adult laughter was too much for her. She couldn't stand the thought of me being happy without her for three seconds.

Shanee was on her feet. "Do you want me to get her?"

"Just mind her head," I said. "Her neck's still a little wobbly."

"Thanks for reminding me," said Shanee.

When she came back with Shinola, she was telling her all about her new job.

"So, I'll be able to get you something really special for your first Christmas," she was telling her. "But that's not the best part. The best part is that I've seen some really cool guys in there, buying incense and stuff."

I loved the way she talked more to Shinola than she did to me.

"Do you think she's grown?" I asked. "I think she's grown a lot. Half her clothes don't fit her any more."

Shanee leaned her head close to Shinola's like they were conspirators or something.

"In fact," she told her, "there's even a very cool guy who works there. He came in as I was leaving."

"The doctor said I can start her on solids soon."

"Your pan's boiling." Shanee sat down with Shinola. "And I get paid for being there and I get a discount as well. I can't believe my luck."

I stared into the fridge. The fridge could've been in a war zone, too.

"I've run out of milk," I announced. And everything else. There was nothing in the fridge but an egg box (without any eggs), a couple of bendy carrots, half a tin of spaghetti and an empty bottle of ketchup.

"S'all right," said Shanee. "I never take milk at home because there's always pieces of spat-back food in it."

I gazed into the tea caddy. I seemed to have run out of tea, too. When had that happened? I was sure there'd been tons left. Shinola and I had done a shop at the beginning of the week. Hadn't we? I remembered walking down the high street. I remembered looking in the windows of the clothes shop and the shoe shop ... but I didn't remember going into the supermarket.

"And guess what else?" said Shanee.

There weren't any cups.

I mean, there *were* cups, but they weren't all in

the kitchen, and the ones that were in the kitchen weren't really clean. I yanked a couple from the sink.

"I can't guess," I said. "My brain's geared for baby things."

Plus, I was distracted. I was having trouble rinsing the cups because there were a few other things in the sink and there wasn't much room.

"Amie's brother's going to take driving lessons," said Shanee. "Then they're going to save up for a car."

I stood in front of the cups so she couldn't see me using one old tea bag for both of us. "Really?"

I took down the tin we kept the biscuits in, but there was nothing in it but a handful of crumbs. I couldn't have done a shop.

"Then maybe next summer we can all go to her parents' cottage in Suffolk for a week. All on our own," Shanee went on. "Won't that be brilliant?"

I could tell that when she said "we" she wasn't including me. Which was fine. I wouldn't be able to go anyway. Even if Les didn't mind – since by then we'd have our own flat and be together – I wasn't going to be the kind of mother who went off with her friends the way Hilary used to go off with Charley whenever she liked.

I put the mugs on the table. "I think I'm going to teach Shinola to swim in the summer," I told Shanee. "The baby book says infants can learn to swim painlessly."

I couldn't really swim myself. But I liked wearing swimsuits. I wouldn't mind sitting by the edge of the pool, watching Shinola amaze everybody by being able to swim before she could walk.

"I've heard—" Shanee began. But as soon as I sat down Shinola started whingeing and she broke off. "I think she wants her mum," Shanee finished.

She blew on her tea while I struggled with Shinola. "Anyway, we might even go to France for a day, as well. If they get a car that can go that far."

Shinola was wide awake by now. I tucked her against my hip so I could more or less hold her steady.

Shanee fished something out of her mug.

"So, what've you been up to?" she asked. "I thought you were going to ask me to mind Shinola when you wanted to go out."

"I don't really feel like going out," I lied. I did feel like going out, and Les asked me to go bowling and stuff like that, but he never gave me enough notice to ask Shanee. Not that I was going to admit that to Shanee. She was always probing about Les, as if she didn't like him or something. Which was really stupid, since she'd never met him. "My domestic side is taking over." I fished something out of my mug. "Les says he can't believe I'm pretty *and* a mother type."

Shanee smiled. "We're all going ice-skating on Saturday if you want to come."

I gave her a look. "With Shinola?"

Shanee shrugged. "I thought maybe Les could look after her for a couple of hours. Give you a break."

"I don't need a break," I said quickly. "I've never been happier." I bounced Shinola on my knee. "As far as I'm concerned, this is what life is all about. Anyway, Saturday's no good for Les. He's really busy at weekends."

Shanee stopped staring into her tea to see what else was in there and stared at me.

"Well, what about Saturday night?" she pushed. "Gerri's parents are away for the weekend and she's having a party. Shinola could sleep in one of the bedrooms."

The thought of being at a party *with* Shinola was even worse than the thought of being at a party *without* Les.

"What about New Year? My mum and her new bloke are taking the brats to Wales straight after Christmas and I'm allowed to have some friends over."

I laughed. "*Your* mother has a bloke?"

I'd never seen Shanee's mother with her hair combed, never mind make-up. Who'd be interested in *her*?

Shanee grinned. "It's wild, isn't it? But you know what the best part is? Derek's a dentist. Can you believe it? They met in an Oxfam shop. They were both after the same jacket."

I couldn't believe that a dentist would fall for a woman with four kids whose idea of getting dressed up was to wear a flannel shirt over her T-shirt and jeans.

I sighed. "Christ… Things don't always turn out like you think they will, do they?"

"Almost never," said Shanee. "But the point is, that gives you plenty of time to sort out a baby-sitter." She looked so chuffed you'd think she'd won the lottery. "Derek's even giving me money for food. Isn't that excellent?"

"For God's sake, it's only November, Shanee. I can't think that far ahead." I was barely able to think about tomorrow, I was always so worn out by today.

Shinola's fist swung out to knock my mug off the table and spill weak but scalding tea over both of us, but I managed to grab her just before she made contact.

"Me and Shinola live one day at a time."

If you could call it living.

Shanee's eyes sort of darted around the room. I could tell that she didn't call it living either, but all she said was, "Well, as far as the rest of the world is concerned, the holiday season has already begun." She grinned. "Party, party, party… Be there or be square…"

"I don't know…"

Even though I hadn't thought about it, I knew I wanted to spend New Year's Eve with Les. He had a green linen suit he bought in the sales that he wore for special occasions. I hadn't seen it, but he'd told me all about it. I reckoned I'd get something blue to complement it. Les wouldn't want to hang out in a council flat with a bunch of teenagers, but maybe we could drop by for half an hour. So everyone could get a good look at him and eat their hearts out. It didn't matter any more if he found out I was younger than he thought. He was going to find out when we went for our marriage licence anyway, wasn't he?

"I'll have to check with Les. He may have other plans."

Shanee scraped some dried formula from the table with a long purple nail. I'd had to cut all my own nails short so I didn't stab Shinola.

"I thought Les went to his mother's for Christmas," said Shanee. "In Norfolk."

"Norwich," I corrected. "But that was last year. This year he may not go."

He hadn't actually said he wouldn't, but I couldn't believe he'd want to miss his daughter's first Christmas. Not even if his mother did make the best fruit-cake in Britain.

"Whatever," said Shanee. "Let me know."

Now that she'd brought it up, Christmas was stuck in my mind. I had this flash of me and Shinola in identical outfits, sitting around the tree with Les. I could always get a fruit-cake from Marks and Sparks.

"What do you think about me and Shinola dressing alike for Christmas?" I dug my spoon in the sugar and lifted it towards my mug. "I saw this picture in one of the Sundays and the mother and daughter both had the same velvet and lace dresses."

Shinola squirmed and the sugar went flying.

"I think oilskin might be better," said Shanee. "Or plastic. Something that's easy to clean." She sipped her tea. Carefully. "So..." She smiled encouragingly. "How's it going?"

"Fine. Everything's brilliant. It's bliss having the old cow out of the house. Every day's a holiday." I smiled to prove how happy I was. "How about you?"

"Great." Shanee's head bobbed up and down. "School's a lot of work, but I'm enjoying it and it's going well. And now that Lucy's got Derek I've got more time for myself. That's why I can take this job."

"That's brilliant."

It was also ironic. It used to be Shanee who could never do anything because she was stuck in the flat helping her mum and I was the one who was always on the go. Now Shanee had *more* time and I had none. Not even just *less* but none. I was still holding Shinola's soppy little fist, but I must've squeezed it too hard or something because she started howling.

"I'll tell you what," said Shanee. "If you and Les want to go somewhere nice, there's this really cool restaurant down near Leicester Square. You'd really like it. They've got parrots and everything."

There'd definitely been a lot of changes in Shanee's life in the last couple of months. The only place she'd ever been at Leicester Square before was the tube.

"Shh…" I hissed at Shinola. "It's not time for your bottle. Let me and Shanee talk."

Shanee, who grew up in a house where quiet was when only three people were shouting, kept on talking.

"It was Edna Husser's birthday," she informed me. "She took ten of us there for supper."

I didn't know who Edna Husser was. She must be new. But I wasn't all that interested just then. As per usual, Shinola'd decided to give it her all. I'd've squeezed her again if it wouldn't've made it worse.

"And then we went to that virtual reality thing."

"Shinola," I begged. "Please… Why don't you give Shanee a big smile? Show her what a good baby you can be…"

They call it projectile vomiting for a reason.

Shanee wiped it off her hand with a bib that was so dirty you couldn't tell if it was decorated with rabbits or bears.

"I'd better get going." She pushed back her chair. "I've got a ton of homework. I'll give you a ring later on, all right? After Shinola's asleep."

She'd be lucky.

Shanee never rang. For days after her last visit I rushed to the phone every time it rang, but it was never Shanee. Sometimes it was my nan or

Charlene, and a couple of times it was Dara on her mobile, ringing on her way to a meeting or a business dinner, but most of the time it was the same person. The last person on earth I had anything to say to. Hilary Let-me-run-your-life Spiggs.

"So how are you doing?"

"About the same as I was doing when you rang last time. Just blooming fine."

"How's the housekeeping money holding out?"

This was something Hilary asked every time she phoned, as if she was programmed, and it was also a trick question. If I told her the truth – that if it wasn't for my Child Benefit and the fifty quid my nan sent me in case I wanted to buy myself a treat, and the fifty quid Dara sent me so I'd have some extra money for Christmas, and the twenty-five quid Charlene sent me for Shinola, I'd have about fifty pence to my name – she'd've done her impersonation of Hurricane Mitch.

"Just great," I assured her. "Everything's brilliant. I should get my first giro soon."

"And how's Shinola?"

"She's brilliant, too."

I could hear her sigh.

"Charley's doing a job up in Camden," my mother went on. "We were thinking he could pick you two up on his way home one night and you could come down for supper. You could spend the night if you wanted, or he could run you home afterwards."

This was another irony. When we lived together she was always shouting at me, and now that she didn't live with me she was always trying to get me to go down for a visit. I reckoned she just wanted to check up on me. You know, make sure I hadn't been beating the baby or taking drugs or something.

"We'd love to," I lied. "But I'm pretty busy this week."

"Next week then."

"I'll have to see how things go."

There were a few seconds of silence that I took to be defeat. But it wasn't. It was her regrouping.

Hilary Spiggs cleared her throat. "Mrs Mugurdy says she's seen your boyfriend a couple of times."

It was just as well I didn't go out much. Mrs Mugurdy probably had a key so she could go through the flat when I wasn't in to make sure I wasn't trashing the place.

"Mrs Mugurdy should mind her own business, *too*," I told her.

"She said he seems very nice," said my mother.

I couldn't believe it. Maybe she missed me – or maybe just missed the flat – but she was ready to make peace. This was her way of giving up. Mrs Mugurdy obviously reported back that Les not only didn't have face piercings or a motorcycle, but that he had a nice car and dressed well and was very polite. Hilary Spiggs was relieved.

But I wasn't going to fall into her trap and say anything more about Les. I knew her. If I said he was nice, within five minutes she'd have his name, address, and NHS number.

I said, "Um…"

"I hope he's contributing," said my mother.

I didn't say anything.

"Well?" she persisted. "Is he contributing?"

If I said yes, I wouldn't be able to come up with some unexpected expense to get some more money out of her. If I said no, she might forget how nice Mrs Mugurdy said he was and lie in wait to confront him herself.

"Of course he is," I assured her. "He's not a wanker."

"That I already know," said my mother.

Nothing to do and Nowhere to do it

I was feeling kind of down by December.

All of a sudden, everybody was *really* busy. Now that he was a manager on a distant planet, Les had even less free time than he'd had before. Shanee'd started going out with the guy from the shop, so she didn't have a minute. Charlene never had any time, and now she had less because she was organizing the school's Christmas fair. Dara was in New York. My nan usually rang every day or two, but Christmas is a big time for quilters and she hadn't rung for a week. Even Hilary was too busy to check up on me much. It made me feel really lonely, with only Shinola to talk to day after day. And only Shinola things to do.

Plus, things weren't going exactly right.

My giro still hadn't come through, and I'd had a letter from the council, reminding Mrs Spiggs that the rent was overdue. I barely had enough left to cover it. I splurged on our velvet dresses for Christmas, but I reckoned they were worth it because we'd wear them for Les. Aside from them, though, I didn't know where the money went, but it went there faster than Concorde. And it wasn't like I was living it up or anything. I'd been existing on Kwik Save No Frills beans and Kwik Save No Frills bread for weeks. I hadn't had any Coke for a month. To economize.

I was still trying to work out how to pay the phone bill when the nurse at the well-baby clinic shouted at me because of Shinola's nappy rash. She said it was practically terminal. She didn't even give me a chance to explain that the reason Shinola's bottom looked like pizza was because I was so broke and had to save on nappies. She piled on the guilt.

"You young mothers seem to think babies are dolls," she snarled. "But if you break a leg off her you're not going to be able to glue it back on."

The day after that, I saw the housing officer. He had a face that looked like it never smiled. He said I wasn't exactly homeless or desperate, was I? He said I had less points than a bowl of jelly and he put me on the bottom of the list. He said to let him know if my circumstances changed.

"You mean, ring you if I die?" I asked.

"Something like that."

After I saw the housing officer, I went home and cried. I just sat on the sofa with my jacket on and Shinola gumming my finger and wept. I really wished Shanee would come over like she used to, and we'd get a couple of bags of crisps and some chips and a few videos and sit up half the night just talking. But the thought of videos made me cry even more. For a few minutes I felt really angry. So angry I took Shinola's giraffe from where it was poking into my bum and hurled it at the telly.

But I didn't exactly know who I was angry with. It wasn't Shanee. And it definitely wasn't Les. I mean, it wasn't Les's fault that he was so good at his job he'd been made the youngest manager in the nation, maybe even in the world. It wasn't his fault that he got transferred to Finsbury Park. It wasn't his fault that Hilary didn't leave me enough money to live on. I could hear the Spiggs say, "But it is his fault you got pregnant," and then I knew who I was angry with.

I could see now that Hilary had planned the whole thing. She knew what having a baby was like. How hard it was to look after one on your own with no one to ever help you out or mind her for a few hours. She knew how much it cost. She knew my friends were all going to be tied up with school and have no time for me. She *wanted* everything to fall apart. She was waiting for me to beg her to come back. She was waiting for me to say that she'd been right and I'd been wrong. But I wasn't going to. I was going to pull myself together and go on. I'd had a couple of temporary setbacks, that was all. Minor, temporary setbacks. The only thing that could really ruin my plans was if me and Les broke up. And that was never going to happen.

But not having any money was a problem. I had nine people to buy Christmas presents for, not counting Les and Shinola. I didn't want to make Hilary think I wasn't coping by turning up with nothing.

I took another Rolo from the packet. I was meant to be eating them slowly because they were a treat. Sort of like a gift from God. I'd gone to the newsagents for a box of matches because the pilot light wasn't working on the stove. I couldn't be bothered putting Shinola in her buggy, so I just carried her to the shop in my arms. The shop was busy and, as per usual, Shinola was whingeing. I was trying to shut her up while we waited in the queue by showing her the sweets on the counter.

I shook a box of Maltesers. "Look," I said. "What's that, Shinola?"

Shinola didn't like the Maltesers.

I picked up a packet of Smarties and shook that.

She didn't like them either.

I'd just picked up the Rolos when an old lady came out from the back of the shop and asked who was next.

The woman behind me gave me a shove. "That's you."

"A box of matches, please," I said, and I shoved my hand in my pocket for the money.

It wasn't until we were outside that I realized that at the same time as I'd gone for the change, I'd stuck the Rolos between me and Shinola.

I was looking at them now the way I'd looked at them then. With wonder.

Then I'd been wondering if I should take them back.

Now I was wondering if I could do it again.

It didn't take me long to work out that I could do it again. And again. And again.

It was a hell of a lot easier than taking a bottle from a hungry baby, I'll tell you that. Especially if you have a baby to help you.

It took me about three minutes to work out that supermarkets were the easiest places to nick things from. And because it was Christmas there was more to nick than tins of soup. Hilary moaned and groaned every year when they changed all the aisles round to fit the stuff for Christmas in. "Where the hell have they put the eggs?" she'd shriek. "Why can't they leave things where they were?" But the extra aisles of gifts and chocolates were the answer to my prayers. It was convenient, one-stop shopping as far as I was concerned.

I was really careful, of course. The last thing I needed was to get me and Shinola arrested. Hilary Spiggs would throw a major fit if her granddaughter ended up behind bars. She probably wouldn't be too happy about me being behind bars, either. A disadvantage of being sixteen that I hadn't thought of before was that now they *could* put me in prison.

Shinola and I went to the shops we always went

to. Everybody knew us 'cause I always chatted to the people on the tills about Shinola and the weather and stuff like that. It was the only adult conversation I had, not counting Les and the occasional phone call from Shanee or a close female relative. I reckoned they wouldn't be watching me because they *knew* me. They'd just think, oh there's that girl and her adorable baby, and never even suspect. Plus, I always bought something. That way, if I did get caught, they'd believe me if I said it was a mistake. "Oh, my God!" I'd cry. "I forgot all about *that*. It was caught in the baby's blankets." And we never went to the same shop twice in a row. We spread ourselves around.

I had almost everything in less than a week. Chocolates for my nan and Charlene's kids, aftershave for each of the men, bath oils for my sisters and the Spiggs, and a stuffed toy for Shinola.

There was only one present I needed that couldn't be had in a supermarket. And that, of course, was Les's. I would've waited till after Christmas Day, to see if someone gave me some money, but Les was going to Norwich to visit his mum on Christmas Eve, so I couldn't put it off.

What I wanted to get Les was a gold I.D. bracelet that I saw in the Argos catalogue. I was going to have his initials engraved on the front and *Love, Lana* on the back. Only now I couldn't even afford the one in the pawnshop with someone else's initials on it.

My second choice was a pair of Tazmanian

Devil socks I'd seen on Oxford Street. Les loved Taz. He even had a Taz air freshener in his car. It wasn't a *great* present, but I reckoned it was a thoughtful one.

It took me a while to work up my courage for this. Shop assistants on Oxford Street were programmed to look out for shoplifters, and you could never completely get out of their view or away from the cameras. Plus, I couldn't afford to buy *anything*, not unless they had some socks on sale for fifty pence.

I filled a couple of old Body Shop and Miss Selfridge carrier bags with stuff of mine, you know, so they'd *think* I really was shopping, but I was counting on Shinola. She was the one who would have to create the distraction.

For once Shinola did what I wanted her to do. The second we walked into the shop she started howling. I leaned over her buggy to comfort her, but she wasn't having any of it. There were a couple of other customers and two salesgirls in the shop, and they all gave me sympathetic smiles. I tried rocking the buggy, but the shop was so small that I couldn't help bumping into things. I kept apologizing and trying to calm her down. I became frazzled and distressed. I lifted her out, blankets and all.

"Please, love…" I begged loudly. "We have to find something for your dad."

Everybody else became frazzled and distressed, too. One of my fellow shoppers fled and the other grabbed a pair of boxers and a scarf and raced to the till. I slipped the socks into Shinola's quilt and stuck her back in her buggy.

Still projecting, the way they taught us to in drama, I said, "We'll have to go if you're going to carry on like this. We'll come back tomorrow."

And that was that: a piece of cake. Chocolate with cherries on top.

I turned the buggy round and started towards the door.

"I'll be back," I promised the salesgirls.

They smiled and waved and called back "Bye" and "See you later."

But just as I got to the door my luck changed.

A group of girls, weighed down with about a dozen carrier bags each, charged in. They were giggling insanely over something. I was about to push past them when I realized who they were.

I was astonished. That's the only word for it: astonished. I mean, how many shops are there in London? Thousands? Tens of thousands? Tens of thousands of shops and twenty-four hours in a day, and at exactly the same time as *me*, Shanee, Gerri and Amie are overcome by an irresistible desire to buy socks on Oxford Street. There must be a God; this sort of thing couldn't happen without planning.

"Lana!"

"Lana!"

"Lana!"

Shinola, taking her cue from God, went as quiet as a flower. The little treasure. I could've thrown her through the window.

"Shanee! Gerri! Amie!" I shrieked back. "What are *you* doing here?"

"Christmas shopping," said Shanee.

"This is the last stop," said Amie. "I'm shopped out."

Gerri laughed. "You're never shopped out till you're dead."

"What about you?" asked Shanee. She gave me a smile. "Looking for something for Dad?"

I smiled back. "Yeah, only Shinola's been fussing, so I'm taking her home."

Amie made a face at Shinola, who, leaving my script completely, smiled back and gurgled.

"She seems all right now," said Gerri.

"We won't be long," said Shanee. "Why don't you wait and we can all go home together?"

It was like robbing a bank and then staying to chat to one of the cashiers.

I nodded at Shinola. "This good mood is just temporary, believe me. You don't want to go home with us, it's a traumatic experience."

"We'll take our chances." Shanee suddenly dropped down and stroked Shinola's cheek. "You're not going to make a scene on the bus, are you, sweetie?"

"I'll just be a second," said Gerri. "I know exactly what I want."

Amie started looking at the boxers, but Shanee kept talking to Shinola. She undid one of the snaps on her jacket. She picked up the toy Shinola had with her and shook it in front of her face. She said, "I think she wants a cuddle." She undid the seatbelt and lifted Shinola into the air.

It happened so fast that I couldn't stop her. One minute Shanee was squatting by the buggy, and the next she was standing on her feet with Shinola in her arms.

The Tazmanian Devil socks fell to the floor.

"What's that?" said Shanee.

"What's that?" said the cashiers.

It was lucky I was born to be an actress as well as a mother.

"Oh, my God!" I slapped my hand across my mouth in stunned surprise. "I forgot all about them! Shinola was crying so much – I must've dropped them in her blanket when I was trying to quiet her."

The salesgirls laughed.

"It's all right," said the oldest. "You definitely had your hands full."

Shanee was still talking to Shinola.

"Is this what you're giving your dad for Christmas? He's going to love these!"

"Do you want to bring them over to the till?" said the salesgirl.

I wasn't sure what to do. Tell her right off that I'd changed my mind? Or act like I was going to buy them and then pretend that I'd lost my money?

"You still want them, don't you?" she pushed.

I could feel everybody looking at me.

"Oh, yes," I said. "Of course I want them."

Amie sidled up next to me. "What's going on?" She gave me a wink. "What've you been doing, Lana? Thieving again?"

It was a joke. I knew it was a joke. And everyone else knew it was a joke, too. Only nobody actually laughed.

Shanee thrust the socks at me. Her fingers closed around my hand and squeezed hard.

"Here you go." She bent down and put Shinola back in her chair. "Let's get this show on the road."

I could feel something that wasn't socks against my palm. I glanced down. There was a twenty-pound note pressed against them.

"It's lucky you found them," I said to Shanee.

Shanee nodded. "Yeah," she said. "I reckon it is."

Usually the thought of spending an entire day with all my family appealed to me about as much as spending an entire day in a maths class. But I was on my own so much that I was almost looking forward to Christmas. At least it'd be warm – Charlene's heating wasn't on a meter, and even if it was she would always have enough money to recharge the key. And there'd be lots of food. And presents. And it was something to wear our new dresses for.

Shinola's velvet dress was green and mine was red. They both had lacy white collars and cuffs. I even dug out the jewellery kit Hilary gave me one

Christmas. I could never be bothered to give it a go, but it was actually pretty good. It had tools, wire, thread, some chains and an assortment of beads. The chains were cheap, but they looked all right from a distance. I shortened one of the gold ones to fit Shinola and I hung a tiny teddy and a star from it. I put the charm Les gave me for Christmas (a teapot this time) on my gold bracelet. So me and Shinola had one image. If we didn't look like mother and daughter, we did look like elves.

As soon as I walked through the door, Charlene scooped Shinola out of my arms.

"The guest of honour has arrived!" she shouted.

My nan came out of the kitchen like a thief leaving a robbery.

"Give her to me!" she ordered and snatched her away from Charlene before Charlene could argue.

I didn't have to think about Shinola for the rest of the day. Everyone wanted to hold her and play with her. The kids wanted to feed her. Nan even wanted to change her. You'd think I'd brought the baby Jesus instead of Shinola Spiggs.

There was food all over the place. Crisps and chocolates. Nuts and pretzels. Biscuits and chunks of cheese and olives. My stomach wasn't growling, it was echoing. I chose a seat where I could reach the nuts and the cheese.

"Here you go," said Justin.

I looked up to find he was handing me a glass of

champagne. I didn't mean to look at Hilary, but it was sort of an automatic response.

"Well, you'll want to join in the toast, won't you?" said my mother.

"OK, now that everybody's here, it's music time!" cried Dara, and she raced to the stereo before anyone could beat her to it. "Then we can open our presents."

"Oh, please," we all begged. "Not Phil Spector."

"It isn't Christmas without the Ronnettes," said Dara.

"That calls for another round," said Mick.

Everybody laughed and held out their glasses. Including me.

Everybody made a big deal of the presents from me and Shinola, even though they weren't much. It was lucky I'd got an extra aftershave for Charley, just in case, since they hadn't split up this year. The Spiggs always told everybody how I gave her a tin opener for her birthday when I was seven, but even she acted like we'd given her a dream trip to Hawaii this year.

"Why, this is lovely, Lana." She actually sounded *sincere*. "Thank you... They're my favourite."

Shinola got a ton of clothes. Most of it was at least six months too big. So she'd have something to grow into. It was kind of scary that the Spiggs, my nan and my sisters all thought the same like that. She also got a ton of toys. All the stuff from Hilary and Charley and Charlene and Dara was educational. My nan gave her a teddy that was nearly as big as I was.

"Where's it supposed to sleep?" I asked. "In *my* bed?"

"It isn't easy to be called Mum," said my nan.

And, except for the quilt Nan made me, all the stuff for me was pretty much for Shinola, too. Charlene and Justin gave me a mobile phone with twenty quid prepaid on it, so I could walk around the flat and talk on the phone at the same time.

"In case there's some emergency," said Justin. "You should have a phone nearby at all times."

"We didn't even have a phone when I was a girl," said Nan. "And my mother had seven of us."

Dara and Mick gave me a subscription to some mother and child magazine and a gift certificate for Mothercare in case there was stuff I needed for Shinola.

"But this is for a hundred pounds!" I knew Mick made a lot of money doing something in the City – and Dara made a lot of money doing something all over the world – but a hundred pounds! They'd never've given me that much to spend on myself.

"Babies grow fast," said Dara. "They always need something."

Charlene's kids, Drew and Courtney, gave me a set of *Sesame Street* videos.

"Wow," I said. "Just what I always wanted."

"Try this then, why don't you?" said my mother.

She handed me a long white envelope with a red bow stuck on it.

I took it without much enthusiasm. You can't fit much in an envelope.

"What is it?"

"That's the idea of opening it," said my mother.

Nobody spoke while I opened the envelope. Even Shinola was quiet.

I removed the papers folded inside.

"It's the lease." I looked up at Hilary. "The lease to the flat."

The Spiggs smiled. "That's right."

I looked back at the lease. It couldn't mean what I thought it meant. I looked back at the Spiggs. Could it?

"I've asked your mother to make an honest man of me," said Charley. He put his arm around my mother.

Hilary patted his knee. "And since it seems a shame to waste two houses on us, I've said yes."

"You're getting *married*?"

What irony! My mother was getting married before *me*.

"Not for a while," said my mother. "But I'll be moving in officially right away. Permanently." She smiled. "Now that you're grown up."

"Isn't that great?" said my nan. "Now you don't have to wait on a council list for the next ten years. You're entitled to your mother's flat. It's in the lease."

Hilary laughed. "Well, say *something*, Lana. Aren't you pleased?"

I just kept staring at the lease like it was Dorothy's ruby shoes.

"Of course I'm pleased."

I was beyond pleased. About a dozen songs were playing in my head at once. After all my disappointments, everything was going to turn out exactly as I'd planned.

The rest of them all started talking at once. Mick was trying to work out exactly how much money I'd have with my Income Support and my Child Benefit and my Housing Benefit, banging on about making a budget for me. He said it was an important lesson in economics. Nan was going on about how I'd be able to go back to school once Shinola was older, and maybe even get a part-time job. Justin didn't think I'd have to wait that long. He thought the government had special programmes for girls in my position with crèches and stuff. Dara reminded me how she paid for her degree in business studies by cleaning houses. Charlene said I should find other young mothers in my area and form a baby-minding club where we each took a turn so the others could have a few hours off. "It's important you have some time for yourself," said Charlene.

I let them talk. It was like having a shower in words. They all ran off me and disappeared.

I nodded and smiled, but I wasn't really listening to any of them. I was listening to the songs in my head.

It was true what everybody always said about things being darkest before the dawn. Here I'd been feeling down and lonely, and all the time every problem I had was about to be solved. The flat was mine! My very own! Now Les could move in and we could live happily ever after.

Nan held up her glass. "A toast!" she cried. "To the best of New Years."

One song separated itself from all the others and kicked into stereophonic. "Just blahblah and me … and baby makes three… We're happy in … my … blue … hea-vennn…"

I raised my glass. "To the best of New Years!"

Happy New Year to Us

I was almost tempted to go home with Hilary and Charley and stay with them till after Boxing Day. They wanted me to. Well, they wanted Shinola to. Even Charley. They couldn't leave her alone. Here I was trying to teach her not to expect to be picked up every time she cried, and there they were, practically arm-wrestling over which one was going to hold her. But I had too much to do to waste time with them. I was full of plans and energy again. Hilary and Charley were coming to move the rest of her stuff in the week, but I said I'd start packing things up before then. I couldn't wait to get started. The sooner she was really out, the sooner I was really in and my life could finally begin properly.

And, of course, there was Les to tell. He'd probably ring on Boxing Day to wish me a Merry Christmas, after his mother had calmed down from the excitement of having him home for a week. I was going to be there when he did.

I spent Boxing Day waiting for Les's call, but it never came. I reckoned his mother must have dragged him off to relatives, so he never had a chance. The first thing the next morning I tied Hilary's books in bundles and put everything that wasn't breakable into black bin liners. I got so involved in packing that I didn't realize Les hadn't rung till ten o'clock that night, when I finally collapsed. I was lying there, surrounded by all the garbage Hilary Spiggs had collected over the years, imagining the flat the way it was going to be. The walls and the furniture were white. There was a set of those stackable glass and chrome tables beside the leather sofa. The coffee table was big and round and also made of glass and chrome. The lights had frosted glass shades and pointed at the ceiling. Les was in our blue and yellow kitchen, making us a nightcap. He sat beside me and handed me my glass. He kissed my cheek. He raised his glass. "Merry Christmas, baby," he whispered. "And a Happy New Year." That was when I realized that he hadn't rung. I was almost too tired to care.

"He'll ring," I told myself as I pulled my new quilt around me. "Probably when Hilary and Charley are here."

I pushed Les out of my mind. I knew what his mother was like. She was a clinger. Plus, she'd have about a million things for him to do in her house when he was there. Plus, he had a couple of aunts and uncles to see. He was probably too busy to get to a phone. Since he couldn't use hers 'cause her income was fixed.

But I was busy, too.

Hilary and Charley came two days after Boxing Day.

"Well, you've certainly been busy," said Hilary, looking round. "I hope you don't dance on my grave as fast as this."

Even though I'd packed up tons of her junk, it took the three of us the whole day to finish sorting all her stuff and loading the van.

Then I threw myself into cleaning the flat with every bit of energy I had left. I worked like a woman possessed, dusting, hoovering, mopping and hauling furniture. By the time I was done, I had blisters on my hands, two splinters and a cut on my forehead from walking into a shelf.

I'd literally just put the hoover away when the doorbell rang.

Tomorrow was New Year's Eve. Which meant it couldn't be Shanee. Shanee'd be running around getting ready for her party.

It had to be Les. That was why he hadn't rung, because he was going to surprise me by turning up for New Year's Eve.

I practically tripped over myself to get to the door before he could ring again and wake Shinola.

Shanee was standing on the doorstep with her arms full of shopping.

"Don't look so happy to see me," said Shanee. "I can't stay for long."

It wasn't that I wasn't happy to see her. It was just that I'd been about to fling myself into her arms. I put a smile on my face and waved her inside.

"Come on!" I cried. "You're the first visitor to our new flat."

Shanee waggled her eyebrows. "And to think I didn't even know you'd moved. It's been longer than I thought."

"Wait till you hear what happened," I said as I led her inside.

Shanee got as far as the living-room and stopped dead.

"Geez," said Shanee. "It looks like you've been robbed."

"Hilary's moved out for good," I told her. "The flat's officially mine!"

Shanee's eyes moved from one corner to the next. "What's left of it," said Shanee.

"Oh, please... It's not done yet, is it? Wait till I paint it all. It'll look really brilliant. And once I save some money I'm going to go really modern." Hilary was too cheap to even buy a toaster, but I was going to have an all-electric kitchen. "You know, with those hobs that don't look like hobs, and an electric kettle, an electric coffee-maker and an electric toaster. And a microwave, of course."

Shanee kept nodding and looking around.

"Everything will be colour co-ordinated eventually."

Shanee gave me a look. "So does this mean that Les will be moving in?"

"Of course," I said. "It's what we've been waiting for."

"Well, that's really great." Shanee let go of her carrier bags and gave me a hug. "Then he'll be coming with you tomorrow night."

"'Fraid not. He's been held up at his mum's."

Shanee was looking at me the same way she'd looked at me when the socks fell out of Shinola's blanket.

"But you're still coming, aren't you?" she asked. "You have to come."

"I know… I have to meet Guy."

Shanee waved Guy away with one hand. "Not any more. Now you have to meet Andy." She laughed. "I met him on Christmas Eve at Edna Husser's. He's a friend of her brother's."

I had to laugh, too. "You've changed a bit. You never used to go out with blokes at all and now you're running through men like they're traffic lights."

"You know what they say," said Shanee.

"Make hay while the sun shines?" I guessed. It was one of my nan's.

"No," said Shanee. "You're only young once."

I spent most of New Year's Eve day debating whether to go to Shanee's party or not. Should I? Shouldn't I? Should I? Shouldn't I? At about nine o'clock, when everyone on the telly was gearing up for the big hour, I decided that I should. Madonna would have.

But the minute Shanee opened the door I knew that I'd made a mistake.

"Lana!" she shrieked. "I can't believe it! You actually came."

Already I didn't know why I had. One minute I was sitting there on my own in my new, empty flat with nothing to do, listening to the echoes, seeing Les in his yellow shirt dancing like John Travolta. And the next I was getting me and Shinola into our velvet dresses.

"I didn't realize it was casual," I mumbled. From what I could see, lots of the girls were in jeans or leggings with see-through or sequinned tops. And almost all of them were wearing black or grey, or some combination of black and grey. Red was obviously not the in-colour this season.

"You look beautiful," Shanee assured me. "Very *mature*."

I took this to mean "old".

Shanee was wearing a dress for a change, but it didn't have a lace collar and cuffs. It didn't have any collar or cuffs. It was long and gauzy and in layers. The top layer was black but underneath it was purple and, underneath that, red. It was very sexy in a quiet sort of way. I'd never seen Shanee look sexy before. It was a bit of a shock.

"You look pretty mature, too," I said.

Shanee grabbed my arm. "Come on, let's put

Shinola in my room, then I'll introduce you to everyone."

"Right," I said. "Brilliant."

I followed her through the mob. A couple of people looked at me as if I was carrying an orang-utan and not a human baby, but mostly nobody seemed to see me. Nobody waved hello or anything. I recognized a few faces, but not as many as you'd think.

"You've certainly made a lot of new friends since I left school," I joked.

"Yeah," said Shanee. "I suppose I have. There's so much going on."

I laughed. "Yeah, I know." There was a lot going on in my life, too, only it all seemed to be going in a circle.

Shanee giggled. "Who ever thought growing up would be so much fun?"

"Not me," I said.

Shinola, of course, was not about to go to sleep just because I wanted her to. She was in play mode.

"I have to get back to the party," said Shanee. She made a face. "The responsibilities of the host-ess. Come and get me when she's asleep."

"Sure," I said. "If I can still recognize you by then."

I sat on Shanee's bed while I waited for Shinola to nod off. A boy and a girl I didn't know poked their heads in once, looking for the snogging room, but other than that we were on our own.

Being in Shanee's room was like going back in time. She still had every photo we'd ever taken of ourselves stuck around her mirror. And she still had the picture of us with her mum and the kids standing in the rain at Thorpe Park. And the traffic cone we found in the road. And her James Dean poster on the wall. I thought about how many hours of my life I'd spent looking at that poster while me and Shanee talked. Hundreds. Maybe thousands. I could actually *see* us sitting there. We were eating biscuits and spraying crumbs everywhere when we laughed.

Shanee was in a clinch in the kitchen when I finally found her.

She didn't even look embarrassed.

"Lana," she gushed. "This is Andy. Andy, this is Lana."

Andy was possibly the most gorgeous bloke I'd ever seen in real life. He wasn't my type – he had a long ponytail and a nose-ring – but he was incredible to look at. Like a film star. Like Johnny Depp. He had to be at least twenty.

Andy said, "How's it goin', Lana?" And ran one hand down Shanee's side.

"I'll be right out," Shanee promised. She kind of bumped her hip into Andy's hip. "I came in for more food. Amie and Gerri are out there. Ask them to introduce you to anyone you don't know."

"OK," I said. "I'll see you in a bit."

I couldn't get Amie's attention. She was laughing her head off with two boys I didn't know. They didn't go to our school, that was for sure.

I couldn't get Gerri's attention either. She was in the snogging room.

I wandered round, picking at the snacks and smiling as if I was having a good time. I got a beer and tried to mingle. I stood on the edge of a group of people and listened with a smile on my face. But they were all talking about people and things that had nothing to do with me. I got another beer. The beer made me feel a little better. I stood myself in a corner and kind of swayed to the music, like I was waiting for someone to ask me to dance.

And then I spotted Gary Lightfoot over by the drinks table. He used to be in my form. He'd always been a bit gawky and stupid, but he was a friendly face, so I gave him a smile. It was like waving a red flag at a bull. He was beside me so fast I bumped into the wall.

"Lana," said Gary. "Long time no see. How's it goin'?"

I said it was going great. How about him?

"Brilliant," said Gary. "So everything's all right?"

"Yeah," I said. "Everything's great."

He was smiling at me like he was posing for a photograph.

"So," Gary cleared his throat. "Did you have the kid?"

"Yeah," I said. "I had the kid." I nodded towards the hall. "She's sleeping in Shanee's room."

"Brilliant." Gary nodded. "So what's its name?"

"She's a girl," I said. "Her name's Shinola."

Gary's smile started to quiver.

"You what?"

"Shinola. It means beauti—"

"Shinola?" Gary's smile was all over the place. "You mean like the shoe polish?"

"Shoe polish?" I wasn't smiling at all. "What are you on about, shoe polish?"

"Shinola," said Gary. "It's a shoe polish."

"No, it isn't." Not only was I not smiling, I was hardly moving my lips. "It means beautiful morning. In African."

Gary gave up trying not to laugh. "No, it doesn't. It means shoe polish in American."

I was still trying to explain that it meant beautiful morning or something like that in some language when he suddenly grabbed a nearby boy and dragged him into the conversation.

"Jake," said Gary. "Isn't Shinola an American shoe polish?"

Jake grinned. "Can't tell shit from Shinola," said Jake.

Gary started cracking up but I just stood there, looking blank.

"It's a saying. It means you're really stupid," Jake explained. "So stupid you can't tell shit from Shinola."

"I suppose that means it's brown," I said.

Gary spluttered. "Is your baby brown?"

"No," I said. "Not last time I looked."

* * *

219

I didn't feel much like partying after that. I watched Gary and Jake stagger off, still laughing. It'd take them about two minutes to make sure that everybody knew I'd named my baby after a shoe polish that looks like shit. I got Shinola and went home.

I walked through my front door just in time to hear Les say, "Well, Happy New Year! See you soon!" And then the answering machine started to whirr.

I couldn't believe it! I'd been at home practically every minute since Christmas Day and the one time I leave the house he rings! I stood there holding Shinola, staring down at the answering machine. A couple of tears slid down my cheek. But then desperation inspired me and I did something I'd never even thought of doing before. I picked up the phone and dialled one-four-seven-one.

It went so fast I wasn't sure I got the number right. I hung up, got a pen and a piece of paper, and dialled it again.

It wasn't a Norwich number at all. It was a London number.

Les must be at home. He'd phoned me as soon as he got back. He did want to spend New Year's Eve with me. It was his surprise. Me and Shinola still had our coats on. I didn't think twice about it. Thank God my nan'd given me a tenner for Christmas. I just turned right round and went back outside and got a taxi.

I know exactly what I was expecting. I was expecting Les in his yellow shirt with a happy grin on his face and a bottle of champagne.

"I was just about to ring you again," he'd say when he opened the door. "I reckoned you must be putting the baby to sleep."

A woman answered the door. She was about Hilary's age, but her hair was grey. I got this really bad feeling when I saw her. The time me and Hilary got robbed, a coldness came over me the second I stepped through the door. Because there was a cassette on the floor, and I knew it shouldn't be there. That was how I was feeling now. This woman shouldn't be here.

"Yes?" She looked from me to Shinola and back again. "Can I help you?"

"Oh," I said. She was wearing an apron and slippers. It had to be the wrong house. I told the driver Number Seventy-one, but he must've misheard me. And I didn't think to check. "I I'm sorry to bother you… I was looking for Les. Les Craft? He lives on this road."

She smiled very slightly. It was a familiar smile. I could feel myself really start to panic. Trillions of thoughts were shooting through my brain.

"Yes? You're looking for Les?"

No, shrieked one of the voices in my head. Les is looking for me!

"Do you know him?" Maybe she was the mother of one of his flatmates. Or he helped carry her shopping in sometimes. "If you could just point out his house…"

That made her laugh. "I think you could say I

know him. I'm Les's mother. And *this* is his house."
Her eyes moved from me to Shinola. "Are you a
friend of his?"

"Oh…" It was like I had this tower of cards
built up inside of me and someone had taken out
one of the cards at the bottom. Everything was
collapsing at once. I could feel it. I could even see
it. I tried to stop it. "*You're* Les's mum?" I forced
myself to smile. "Les didn't say you were coming
down to London."

She gave me a puzzled look. "But I *live* in London.
Here. I've lived in this house for thirty years."

Crash went why Les never gave me his home
phone number. *Crash* went why his mobile was
never on. *Crash* went why I could never go to his.
Crash went the flu Les had last year. *Crash* went
why he couldn't spend any of Christmas with me.
Crashcrashcrash. But I still tried to stop it.

"But you can't," I blurted out. "Les – I mean, I
thought you lived in Norwich."

"Norwich?" She smiled like she thought I must
be on drugs. "My sister lives in Norwich, but I
live here. With Les." She pushed the door forward
just a bit. "How do you know Les?" She gave me
and Shinola another once-over. "You *are* a friend
of his?"

I was standing on her doorstep with a baby in
my arms on New Year's Eve. What did she think I
was, a Girl Guide? But I couldn't say anything like
that. I knew that once I started, I'd never stop. And
the crashing cards would never stop either.

"Yes," I said. "Of course I am." I bounced Shinola gently in my arms. "A very good friend."

Her smile was polite at first, but now it was just kind of there.

"A very good friend who doesn't know that he lives with his mother?"

"Well, I—" No wonder the kitchen was so tidy. No wonder I never saw any room but Les's. I made my voice not shake. "Is Les at home?"

She held the door steady. "I'm afraid you just missed him." She sounded anything but sorry.

"Well, will he be back soon?"

She shook her head. "It's New Year's Eve." In case I'd missed that. "He's gone to a party."

"Oh, right," I said. "So there's no point in waiting."

"No," said Mrs Craft. "No, there's no point in waiting. I believe he's spending the night at a friend's."

I didn't cry while I was talking to Les's mother, and I didn't cry after she went back inside and turned off the outside light either. I just stood there, staring at the door. It was a wooden door, painted white. It had a brass letterbox and four tiny windows of coloured glass. I stood there until the shock wore off enough for me to feel the cold. Then I turned round and headed home.

There was nothing inside me except this big hole. This big, cold hole. It made me numb from the inside out. I remember looking up at the sky to see if there were any stars, but Dollis Hill wasn't like the hospital ward with its shiny silver stars. The sky was browny pink and blank, as if we were underground.

I don't remember the walk home. Maybe Shinola was awake, and maybe she was sleeping. Maybe we walked on the main road, and maybe we stayed on the side streets. I do remember the Christmas decorations and faraway laughter.

I wasn't scared. There were lots of drunks out, and probably lots of muggers, too, but I couldn't give a used tampon. So what if someone attacked me? What could they do? Beat me up? Kill me? Big deal.

Anyway, I was really sure God wouldn't let anyone rape or murder me. It was too easy. My life was punishment enough.

I was in one of those films I didn't like to watch. The sort of film that Charley liked. He thought they were realistic. "Sit down and watch this with us," he'd say. "This is about real life." But they weren't realistic, they were depressing. They never had happy endings, and most of the time somebody died, or might as well have. Even if they were in colour I always felt like they were in black and white.

And that was me, walking through the dark on New Year's Eve with my baby in my arms and about a trillion things in my mind all at once. All the lies Les had told me. All the half-truths. Even all the truths. Nothing was how I thought it was. And nothing was going to be how I thought it would be. I could see that now. I could see it really clearly. Like I should've seen it all along.

It was like I'd been sleeping for about a hundred years, and now I'd woken up. But it wasn't the Prince's kiss that woke me. It was the toe of his boot in my face.

Les had never really been interested in me. Not *really* interested. Not like I was in him. He probably had another girlfriend. Maybe more than one. That was why he was always so busy. I wondered who he really went to Greece with. Or maybe he went to Greece like he went to Norwich. Maybe he'd been in London all the time. All the time I was sitting in the house on my own. All the time I was in labour. All the time.

I made up our love, I made up our happiness. I made up our future and our present. But of all the things I made up maybe the worst thing was that I made up Les. He wasn't independent. He wasn't going to be a big success. He wasn't even very nice really. He was just OK. He was an OK bloke with a boring job he pretended was important who still lived with his mum. For all I knew, she *did* pick out his clothes. Maybe he didn't even have good dress sense.

I kept hearing Shanee say, *You're only young once... You're only young once...*

Yeah, I thought. And I'd thrown it away. I'd never done anything in my whole life that wasn't a mistake.

I was only young once and now I was old. Five years from now, I'd still be exactly where I was. I'd be scrimping for this and saving for that. I'd be shopping in Kwik Save and charity shops. I wouldn't go to art school like Shanee, or for weekends in the country with my friends. I'd never have my dream house or my dream family. Because that was all they were. Just dreams. My real house was the flat I'd lived in since I was little. My real family was Shinola.

We passed Shanee's on the way up the road. You could hear the music all the way down at the corner. The music and the laughter and the shouting of teenagers who'd had a few drinks and were having a good time. And for a second I could actually see myself in there with them. Not like I was earlier in the evening, but like I should've been. Like who I used to be.

Shinola was crying by the time we got to the flat. I turned the telly on loud so I'd hear another voice and then I got Shinola ready for bed. I did it like I was a robot. Change nappy ... heat bottle ... put on pyjamas...

She took her bottle all right, but she didn't want to be put in her cot. Because I'd been holding her so much.

"Tough titties," I told her. And I slammed the bedroom door behind me.

I could still hear her in the living-room. I turned the telly up even louder and put on the stereo, but I couldn't drown her out. Mrs Mugurdy started doing her dance on my ceiling. I didn't want a fight with Mrs Mugurdy just then. I turned everything down and went back to the bedroom.

I had the hall light on, so I could see her even though the room was dark. I looked down on Shinola, wide-awake and screaming, but what I saw was Les's mother, blocking the entrance to Number Seventy-one and smiling like I was a beggar or something.

She didn't know about me even vaguely. It never occurred to her that I was Les's girlfriend. It never occurred to her that I was holding her grandchild in my arms.

And that's when I finally started to cry.

It was like some giant was shaking me, I was sobbing so much.

What did my life amount to? Bloody nothing, that's what. I had a ratty old council flat that I'd end up dying in, and a baby named after a shoe polish. And it wasn't even British shoe polish.

Shinola cried and I cried. I don't know for how long. And all I wanted was to go back. To go back a year and be Lana Spiggs again, not Shinola Spiggs' mum. That's all I wanted. I just wanted to be where I used to be, with a future.

I stopped crying, but Shinola didn't.

I wished she would go away. Just disappear. Then everything could go back to the way it was. I'd go back to do my GCSEs and go to parties and maybe even go to drama school. Shanee could move in with me and share the flat. We'd be like *Friends*.

Mrs Mugurdy might die and a couple of guys get her flat. Then we'd really be like *Friends*.

Shinola kept shrieking.

"Shut up!" I shouted. "Shut up! Shut up! Shut bloody up!"

But she wouldn't, would she?

"Just go away!" I begged. "Just go away!"

Suddenly I saw how easy it would be to wipe the last year right out of my life. Just put the pillow over her head for a couple of minutes. That was all. Just hold it there.

It wasn't really like I was thinking it, it was like I was dreaming it.

I watched myself pick up the quilt Nan had made her and throw it over Shinola. I watched myself pick up the pillow and put it over her head.

The New Year's chimes started ringing on the telly. Outside I could hear fireworks and people shouting. I pressed down.

One ... two ... three ... four ... five...

One tiny fist poked out from under the quilt and the pillow. It waved in the air.

And I could see her holding on to my hair, the way she always did. She wasn't covered up in the cot, she was in my arms, pulling my hair so much it hurt. I don't know, it just got to me, that's all. It was Shinola's hand, and there was always gunge between the fingers. I remembered counting them in the hospital.

Six ... seven ... eight ... nine...

I could never go back. Unless I got amnesia, I

was never going to be the way I was. If I'd wanted to get rid of Shinola, I should've done it before she was born.

Ten … eleven…

If I wasn't going to go back, then I might as well go forward. I couldn't see that I had much choice.

I threw the pillow and quilt across the room. Shinola was purple and gasping. I was so scared I didn't know what to do. I just stood there hugging her.

Twelve…

I hadn't heard the phone ring but I heard the answering machine pick up.

"Happy New Year, Lana and Shinola!" shouted Hilary and Charley. "Happy New Year!"

Shinola coughed and all this baby snot blew across the front of my dress.

"Well, I guess it's just you and me," I told Shinola.

Shinola's fingers twisted themselves around my hair.

I winced in pain.

"Happy New Year to you, Shinola Spiggs," I said. "Happy New Year to us."

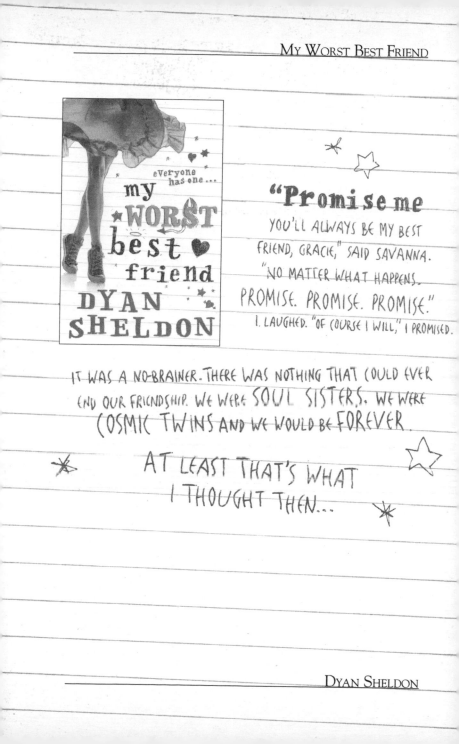

"Promise me YOU'LL ALWAYS BE MY BEST FRIEND, GRACIE," SAID SAVANNA. "NO MATTER WHAT HAPPENS. PROMISE. PROMISE. PROMISE." I LAUGHED. "OF COURSE I WILL," I PROMISED.

IT WAS A NO-BRAINER. THERE WAS NOTHING THAT COULD EVER END OUR FRIENDSHIP. WE WERE SOUL SISTERS. WE WERE COSMIC TWINS AND WE WOULD BE FOREVER.

AT LEAST THAT'S WHAT I THOUGHT THEN...

JUDE MUST GET AWAY

She has to ace her exams and an audition at a prestigious drama school or she'll never escape her small town life and follow her dream of becoming an actor.

WHEN YOUR BEST FRIEND CAN'T LIVE WITHOUT YOU

joanna nadin

wonderland

But then her best friend Stella returns, bringing excitement and danger to Jude's dull existence. For the first time, she can be who she wants to be. But as her life spirals out of control, Jude uncovers a dark secret.

WILL STELLA SAVE HER — OR DESTROY HER?

I USED TO BE SOMEONE.
SOMEONE NAMED JENNA FOX.

A girl wakes from a coma following a
devastating accident, her memory a blank.
One day she can't walk; the next she can.
One day her right eyelid droops; the next it doesn't.
Her parents call her recovery a miracle – but at what
cost has it come? What are they hiding from her?

Who is Jenna Fox?

"A terrific book, overlaid with tension and mystery. I loved it." *Philip Pullman*

the
Uninvited
TIM WYNNE-JONES

When Mimi Shapiro needs to get out
of New York fast, her estranged father's remote
Canadian cottage offers an ideal retreat.

The little house is fairy-tale quaint and the
key is just where her dad promised it would be,
so Mimi is shocked to discover someone already
living there – Jay, a young musician. Jay accuses
Mimi of being responsible for the dead bird and
other threatening tokens left in the house, but
she's only just arrived. So who is the intruder,
and what do they want?